Daisy Redford's Shopping List

Paper towels

Candles (for romance; loved the ones Chance had last night)

Lightbulbs

Panty hose (mine were accidentally left at a certain bachelor's house)

Milk

Orange juice

Eggs (starved—didn't get a chance to eat breakfast; too busy sneaking out of Chance Foster's bedroom)

Shampoo

Toothpaste

Home pregnancy kit (oh, my, something tells me I might be needing this....)

Nail polish remover

Hand lotion

Wedding gown (in case the stick turns blue, a gal's gotta be ready!)

Dear Reader,

May is *"Get Caught Reading"* month, and there's no better way for Harlequin American Romance to show our support of literacy than by offering you an exhilarating month of must-read romances.

Tina Leonard delivers the next installment of the exciting Harlequin American Romance in-line continuity series TEXAS SHEIKHS with *His Arranged Marriage*. A handsome playboy poses as his identical twin and mistakenly exchanges "I do's" with a bewitching princess bride.

A beautiful rancher's search for a hired hand leads to more than she bargained for when she finds a baby on her doorstep and a *Cowboy with a Secret*, the newest title from Pamela Browning. 2001 WAYS TO WED concludes with *Kiss a Handsome Stranger* by Jacqueline Diamond. Daisy Redford's biological clock had been ticking...until a night of passion with her best friend's brother left her with a baby on the way! And in *Uncle Sarge*, a military man does diaper duty...and learns about fatherhood, family and forever-after love. Don't miss this heartwarming romance by Bonnie Gardner.

It's a terrific month for Harlequin American Romance, and we hope you'll "get caught reading" one of our great books.

Wishing you happy reading,

Melissa Jeglinski
Associate Senior Editor
Harlequin American Romance

KISS A HANDSOME STRANGER
Jacqueline Diamond

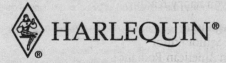

HARLEQUIN®

TORONTO • NEW YORK • LONDON
AMSTERDAM • PARIS • SYDNEY • HAMBURG
STOCKHOLM • ATHENS • TOKYO • MILAN • MADRID
PRAGUE • WARSAW • BUDAPEST • AUCKLAND

Special thanks and acknowledgment are given to Jacqueline Diamond for her contribution to the 2001 Ways to Wed series.

For Sylvia Hyman, ceramic artist and terrific mother

ISBN 0-373-16875-6

KISS A HANDSOME STRANGER

Copyright © 2001 by Harlequin Books S.A.

Visit us at www.eHarlequin.com

Printed in U.S.A.

ABOUT THE AUTHOR

Jacqueline Diamond is the daughter of a ceramic artist who inspired Daisy's talents in this book. Jackie lives in Southern California with her husband, two sons and two formerly stray cats.

AUTHOR'S NOTE: Anyone interested in helping save feral (born-wild) cats, as Frannie and Bill do in this story, can get more information from Alley Cat Allies at 1801 Belmont Road NW, Suite 201, Washington, D.C. 20009. Any mistakes made in describing Frannie and Bill's approach are strictly the author's own.

Books by Jacqueline Diamond

HARLEQUIN AMERICAN ROMANCE

HARLEQUIN INTRIGUE

When three best friends need advice on finding that perfect love match, they turn to the wisest relationship book around, *2001 Ways to Wed*.

Chapter 8
When Smooching Leads to Sleeping Over And Other First Date Debacles

He was gorgeous. The stars were twinkling. He bought you dinner, a movie *and* flowers. You were wearing that little black number that makes you feel sexy. You'd shaved your legs. He asked you up for coffee—and you ended up staying for breakfast.

Heaven knows you're *not* that kind of girl! But does he?

It's understandable that you're embarrassed, but what if you can't avoid seeing him again—you work with the guy, he's your neighbor or your best friend's notorious playboy brother. So what do you do?

It all depends on how you feel about him. When the lust and the Long Island iced tea wore off, was he just another pretty face? If so, chalk it up to a lesson learned. But if there's potential for a lasting relationship, don't let the rapid pace of your first date kill any chance for a second. If he wants to see you again, go. And don't feel like you have to be intimate again. But beware, some men are just so delicious you can't resist going back for seconds....

Chapter One

Daisy Redford smacked Chance Foster a couple of times. Then she pushed him so hard he compressed into a lump of submissive clay.

"Take that!" she told the clay as it spun around on the potter's wheel, perfectly centered.

Some internal demon had goaded her earlier into making a little bust of the man. She couldn't capture the teasing light in his eyes, but, for a quarter-hour's effort, it had been a creditable likeness of his strong face, full mouth and straight nose.

She'd felt a flash of satisfaction when she pounded him into oblivion. Now, though, the only evidence of her triumph was the neatly spinning lump, ready to be made into a pot, and spatters of wet clay that she could feel drying across her cheeks.

Another woman might have washed a man out of her hair. Daisy Redford had smashed him onto the potter's wheel. If her actions stopped the images of their stolen night together from tormenting her dreams, she would be happy. More than happy. Ecstatic.

"Now all I have to do is find Mr. Right before my girlfriends match me up with yet another loser," she announced to her empty studio. "Or before I find another loser on my own."

It was ironic. Her two best friends, Phoebe and Elise, had set out months ago to find Daisy a mate so she could have a child before endometriosis made her infertile. Both had sworn they weren't interested in men for themselves, yet along the way they'd fallen in love and gotten engaged.

Not Daisy. She'd met a guy she thought was terrific, only to learn that he was bad news personified. "And then some," she muttered.

Uh-oh, she was talking to herself. Thank goodness her assistant, Sean, was off on Mondays, when Daisy closed her downtown Phoenix gallery, so there was no one around to hear.

Today no one wandered through the three exhibition rooms or the sales gallery, or examined the photo portfolio of other available works. Today the only activity was confined to one of the two storage rooms, which she had converted to a studio.

Mondays belonged to the artist side of Daisy. She never sold or displayed her own pottery, because she didn't consider it good enough. But she loved making it, and often gave her creations to her friends and her mother.

Now, carefully applying pressure, Daisy drew up a vase from the wet clay on the wheel. Between her steady hands, the material assumed a high-shouldered shape. It was similar to several previously made pots, each about fifteen inches tall, that stood drying on a canvas-covered table.

The small room was crowded with the potter's wheel, a shelf of glazes, several drying tables and an electric kiln. It was, however, well ventilated and well lit.

A faint pounding echoed through the room. It sounded like distant hammering, perhaps repair work at the Civic Center a few blocks away. Not until she stopped the wheel to remove the pot did Daisy realize someone was knocking on the gallery's locked front door.

"Oh, great." She hurried to scrape and scrub clay off her hands, then wiped them on a towel.

There was no time to change her stained canvas shoes or disreputable jeans. Normally, she might have ignored a visitor to the closed gallery, but she was expecting a shipment from one of her artists, and perhaps the driver didn't realize he was supposed to use the alley entrance.

After wiping her feet on a mat, she hurried through the gallery, called Native Art because it represented local artists. Although some of the pottery and weavings did indeed show a Native American influence, the painting and sculpture were contemporary.

Sure enough, through the front window she could see a delivery van double-parked on the street. The man outside wore the uniform of a local trucking company.

Daisy pushed a hank of hair off her forehead and unbolted the door. "You have to deliver through the back."

"Checked your alley recently?" the man demanded. "They're working on the waterline at the end, and there's a van blocking the other. The driver's nowhere around."

"I'm sure he'll be back any minute." She glanced anxiously along the busy street, which was lined with trendy shops and restaurants. At this noon hour, cars and pedestrians bustled by like hungry ants. Double-parking was likely to bring a ticket, and she could just guess who would get stuck paying for it.

"I can't wait, lady," the man said. "Sorry, but I've got another order to pick up this afternoon."

Daisy made a snap decision. Better to unload everything right now than to risk having him depart with an exhibit scheduled to open this Saturday.

"Okay, but you'll have to hurry," she said, and opened the facing door to create a double aperture.

Daisy didn't like going outside in such a messy state. Chance Foster's law office was a block away, and she'd barely avoided running into him several times in the past two months. On the other hand, he didn't know her real identity and, beneath these clay daubs, he wasn't likely to recognize her even if he saw her.

"Be careful!" she told the delivery man, who, with his assistant, was carting a painting-shaped package down a ramp. "Go right through here, all the way to the back."

The dozen acrylic works were heavy, and several had odd-shaped frames. The workmen were none too careful, either, and twice Daisy barely saved potted plants from being knocked over as they trudged through the gallery.

At last, with relief, she made a final check of the truck's interior and found it empty. "Thanks," she said.

The men waved and climbed into the cab. Daisy was almost at the gallery entrance when, half a dozen doors down, a woman emerged from Le Bistro Français.

Honey-blond hair swirled around her pouty face. The bee-stung lips quivered and her wide eyes glistened.

A man stepped out right behind her. Daisy's fists clenched.

Chance Foster radiated good taste, from the elegant cut of his light-brown hair to his expensive business suit. Yet no amount of subdued overlay could disguise the tantalizing leanness of his hips or the masculine way he carried himself.

She knew every inch of him, from those watchful gray eyes and broad shoulders down to the muscular thighs. In spite of her resolve never to have anything to do with Chance again, Daisy wanted him.

She ached not so much for the physical pleasures they'd shared—although those had been amazing—as for the gentle way he'd talked and listened and eased inside her closely guarded heart. Or pretended to, anyway.

A pang shot through her when Chance put his arms around the woman. They stood next to a sleek car, and he held her for several minutes before going to open the driver's door for her.

He stood in traffic, making sure the blonde got inside safely. Daisy hoped the woman wasn't naive enough to think that meant he cared about her. Chance was suave, all right, a perfect gentleman and a charmer. He was also the most notorious playboy in Arizona.

Two long strides carried him to the sidewalk, where he waited until the car pulled away. On the point of turning toward his office, he halted and stared straight at Daisy.

Please don't let him recognize me. She didn't see how he could, with clay hardening across her nose and cheeks. Yet he remained planted there, indifferent to the people flowing around him. Maybe he'd noticed her distinctive, chin-length auburn hair, she realized.

"Oops." Daisy hurried inside and locked the door. She straightened the Closed sign before fleeing to the back room.

Long minutes ticked past. When no one rapped on the glass, she wasn't sure whether to be relieved or disappointed.

She should never have gone to bed with a man she had just met. It wasn't like Daisy. Being an illegitimate child, the daughter of a man who promised the moon and delivered nothing but empty sky, she'd been careful to avoid casual involvements.

But that night at Elise's engagement party, the handsome newcomer had brought to life all her fantasies. He'd put her at ease when they talked, and electrified her when they danced together.

When he invited her to his house for a drink, she'd welcomed the chance to continue their talk. Besides, she hadn't wanted either Elise or Phoebe, the party's hostess, to spoil this magical mood by fussing over them. Her friends sometimes went a bit overboard in their attempts to pair Daisy off.

She could see, in retrospect, how foolish she'd been to abandon her usual caution. Most of the time, when she met a man, the first thing she assessed was what kind of father he would make. Especially since she'd reached the age of thirty and, due to the severity of her condition, had to marry soon or possibly lose her opportunity for motherhood.

With Chance, though, Daisy hadn't worried about such things. She'd simply enjoyed being with him. In his house, in his arms, in his bed.

That evening she'd given him her real name, Deirdre, because it made her feel more sophisticated. When he'd said his name was Charles, she hadn't realized that he, too, was better known by a nickname.

It was after they made love and were talking quietly that she asked how he knew Elise. She'd nearly stopped breathing when he said, "I'm her brother."

Chance Foster was famous. Or, rather, infamous. According to Elise, his conquests included the most attractive women in Phoenix. A different woman for every occasion, that was his reputation.

When she realized who she'd slept with, Daisy could have smacked herself for being such an idiot. Until that moment she'd believed they were special to each other, that their instant rapport had been as exciting to Chance as to her. Now she knew it was a trick he used to wrap a woman around his finger.

She'd waited until he fell asleep, then called a taxi and fled. Now she was cowering in her studio to avoid him, when the man probably hadn't given her a moment's thought in the past two months.

Annoyed at herself, Daisy used a wire to cut the vase's bottom from the mound of clay remaining on the wheel. Carefully she set it on the table to dry.

Who was that woman at the restaurant? she wondered. The make of car, the clothes and the grooming all shouted, Rich! Or, possibly, In debt and loving it!

Without giving much thought to what she was doing, Daisy seized a few pieces of clay, created a woman's features and attached them to the side of a partially dried pot. The resulting face, a caricature of the blond woman, had a hungry, predatory look.

On the vase next to it, she devised Chance's visage with a sly smile and leering eyes. Studying it, she realized she might finally have hit on an individual twist for her work.

"I could make a whole line of Character Crockery," she mused. "Or maybe I should call them Personality Pots."

The prospect appealed to her. Daisy enjoyed fooling around with caricatures in clay, but had never shown them to anyone, let alone considered selling them. People weren't likely to buy little heads with no practical use.

These pots, on the other hand, could hold plants. She smiled. Poison ivy, maybe.

A flame of excitement sprang up. Daisy's ceramic work, although technically accomplished, had until now lacked uniqueness, but this idea was promising. Although other artists had made pots with faces, she knew she could take her idea in new directions.

How ironic that this development had been inspired by Chance Foster!

She spent the rest of the afternoon experimenting with ways to create character faces on her pots. By making slight depressions, she created eye sockets and other contours that gave her work an even more distinctive look.

By late afternoon Daisy's arms ached pleasantly and her agitation over the near encounter with Chance had dissipated. She was cleaning the studio when the phone rang.

"Native Art," she responded.

"Hi, Native, this is Elise!" joked her friend.

How could such a delightful woman have such a heartless brother? Daisy wondered, not for the first time. "What's up?"

"I picked my colors! Deep-rose and pale-yellow!"

Daisy didn't immediately grasp her friend's meaning. Then it hit. "Oh, for the wedding." Elise and her fiancé, James, would be walking down the aisle in September, three months from now. "That sounds lovely."

"You know what this means," Elise said. "We can start looking at bridesmaids' dresses for you and Phoebe."

"Great." Since Elise hadn't wanted to favor one of them as the maid of honor, they were both going to walk down the aisle together. It would be kind of funky, Daisy thought, but fun.

"How about if we meet for a swim right after work? Say, five-thirty?" Elise went on. "We can talk strategy and cool off at the same time."

Although it was only June, temperatures hovered in the high eighties. "Sounds great."

"See you there."

"There" meant the Mesa Blue condominium complex, where the three women lived. The blue-tiled pool, nestled among ferns and a few squatty palms, provided a refreshing meeting place in summer months.

Daisy couldn't wait to take a dip and see her friends. After draping loose plastic covers over the pots to prevent cracking, she hurried home.

CHANCE FOSTER COULD HAVE sworn he recognized the smudged redhead outside the art gallery. By the time he strolled by, though, she'd disappeared and the place was closed.

He stood on the sidewalk like a smitten teenager, debating whether he dared knock. But what would he say? That two months ago he'd spent a wonderful evening with a mysterious woman and now he was trying to find her?

He couldn't understand how such an intriguing woman could get invited to his sister's engagement party without either Elise or Phoebe knowing her. Afterward, both had roundly denied knowing anyone named Deirdre.

Deciding not to waste any more time on a wild-goose chase, he walked back to his office. Still, Chance's mind wouldn't leave the subject.

He told himself for the umpteenth time that he must have been mistaken in his impression of Deirdre. The honest, direct, sunny lady who'd knocked him off balance wouldn't have left without saying goodbye. There must be a darker side to her personality. Or maybe she'd fooled him from the beginning.

Perhaps she was married and cheating on her husband. Or so afraid of commitment that she panicked when she met a guy she might care about.

As a family law attorney, Chance had seen how many things could go wrong in a relationship. A lot of times the problems sprang from a partner who lacked the character to stick around and stay faithful when the going got tough.

He would like to see Deirdre again, though, at least to learn why she'd bailed out on him. And so he could stop imagining he saw her on the street, the way he'd done today and several times previously.

As he reached the professional building, Chance wondered if his sister and her fiancé had followed his advice to get premarital counseling. People as successful as those two—Elise was a French professor, James a wealthy businessman—didn't think they needed any preparation for marriage. But to Chance, that was like someone saying he didn't need medical insurance because he was healthy.

He decided to drop by her condo after work and, as her big brother, take the liberty of nagging a bit.

"I AM NOT GOING TO WEAR a yellow dress!" declared Phoebe. Sitting on the edge of the pool, she swished her feet in the water. "Yellow looks awful on blondes. And rose will do terrible things to Daisy's complexion! I mean, she's a redhead, for heaven's sake."

"I was thinking of the flowers," Elise admitted. "Yellow and red roses would look so pretty in a bouquet."

Daisy tilted her face to soak up the lingering rays of sunshine. With her tendency to freckle, she couldn't enjoy midday sunbathing, so this was a treat.

"Come on, Daisy!" Phoebe prodded her with an elbow. "Back me up, here. Yellow wouldn't look so great on you, either."

Daisy stretched and smothered a yawn. Not that she wasn't vitally interested in her friends' arrangements, but after all, Phoebe was the beauty consultant. She was also studying biochemistry with the goal of establishing her own cosmetics company, and she had a good sense of what colors looked right on people.

Daisy's own taste ran to the offbeat. Her swimsuit, for example, had been created by her mother, Jeanine Redford, a seamstress and costume designer in Tempe.

A single, angled black strap continued as a diagonal black slash across the emerald green stretch fabric of the swimsuit. A geometric cutout at the waist furthered the impact. It wasn't so much a bathing suit as a dramatic statement.

"We could ask my mom," she said. "She'd come up with a memorable design."

Elise grinned. "I love your mother's costumes, but not for my wedding, thank you." To Phoebe she said, "The yellow can go, but I like deep-rose."

Phoebe stood up, a move that displayed her impressive figure to advantage. In fact, the former actress was impressive to look at from any angle.

"I came here to swim, not argue," she said. "First one to reach the far end gets to pick the colors, okay?"

She dived in, water closing over her head with scarcely a ripple. The pool looked so inviting that Daisy jumped in and swam after her friend.

"It's my wedding so I get to choose!" shouted Elise, and made a long arcing dive past Daisy. A few furious kicks carried her past Phoebe, as well, and she arrived at the far end first. "Deep-rose," she reaffirmed when she could speak. "Deep rose and...something."

Phoebe emerged and caught her breath. "Forget rose. How about green?" she said. "Green and gold."

Elise grimaced. "That sounds like pom-poms at a high school football game."

"Purple and white?" Daisy suggested as she paddled alongside.

"That's for a royal coronation," said Elise. "I don't care how rich James is, I don't want anyone thinking I'm turning into a princess."

A burst of meowing drew their attention toward apartment 1B. On the patio, a bevy of cats gathered as a fiftyish woman with unnaturally red hair filled their feeding dishes.

"I wonder how Frannie and Bill are getting along?" Phoebe mused.

Red-haired Frannie, with her brightly colored clothes and beehive hairdo, made an odd contrast to the soft-spoken building superintendent who lived in a nearby unit. The two had been edging toward each other for months and finally seemed to be hitting it off, but had parted after a jealous quarrel.

Apparently Bill had also noticed the cat noises. The

large, usually jovial man, returning from one of his periodic inspections of the premises, stopped near the pool and gazed wistfully toward Frannie.

She ignored him, and after a moment Jeff Hawkin, the handyman, stuck his head out of the laundry room and requested Bill's attention. Daisy hoped they were fixing the number three dryer, which ate quarters.

"Pale-pink might work," Phoebe suggested, returning to their previous conversation.

"Pale pink with what?" Elise asked.

"White?" said Daisy. "No, too boring. How about three colors? Pale pink with black and white?"

"Black? At a wedding?" Elise groaned.

"Let's go try on dresses and figure out what colors look good on us," Phoebe said. "That way Daisy and I can buy something we might actually wear again."

"What if chartreuse looks good on you?" grumped their friend. "Oh, good, here comes big brother. Let's see what he thinks."

To her horror Daisy spotted an all-too-familiar figure strolling from the lobby into the courtyard. It had been sheer coincidence that had kept her from meeting Chance before that ill-fated night of the engagement party. Why couldn't she have the same luck now?

Frantically she gazed around for somewhere to hide. Giving up, she sucked in her breath and sank under the water.

Chapter Two

Chance smiled when he glimpsed his sister and her two friends lolling in the pool. He liked women and enjoyed their company, which was a good thing, since he had seven younger sisters.

He'd scarcely cleared the lobby, however, when a strange-looking woman, standing ankle deep in cats on her patio, regarded him sharply. Her name, he recalled from a previous visit, was Frannie.

"Be careful around those girls," she said. "Two of them are engaged and the other one's peculiar."

"Peculiar?" He wondered what had provoked this unsolicited observation. On the other hand, he had to admit that Elise's disappearing friend Daisy did seem a bit odd. In the few seconds he'd been distracted by the cat lady, the woman he guessed was Daisy had vanished again as if by magic.

He'd glimpsed her once in hair curlers and a globby green face mask, and another time, from the back, in a flimsy bathrobe. Both times she'd fled from Elise's place to her next-door unit without acknowledging him.

"She's an artist," said the woman. "You never see her out painting anything, though. Peculiar, if you ask me. I'd stay clear, if I were you."

"Thanks." He was about to turn away when he caught Frannie's wink. "You're kidding, right?"

"Just wanted to see how much you'd believe!" She chuckled. "You're Elise's brother, aren't you?"

"That's right. And you really had me going." The lady was quite a character, Chance thought in amusement.

Resuming his approach to the pool, he tried vainly to figure out how Daisy could have disappeared so quickly. "Where's your other friend?" he called to Elise.

She pointed into the water. "Drowning." She didn't sound concerned, so he assumed she was kidding. "We need your advice."

"I get paid for my advice." Chance paused a few feet away. "Since you're my sister, I'll work on contingency."

"Don't you think yellow looks horrible on blondes?" said Phoebe. The blond woman was stunning, he noted for the umpteenth time. There'd never been any chemistry between them, though, just friendly banter.

"I refuse to incriminate myself," he said.

"Spoken like a lawyer," said his sister.

"And deep-rose would look simply horrible with...that. Agreed?" Phoebe indicated some reddish brown hair floating on the water, obviously attached to their pal Daisy's head.

"I plead the fifth amendment," Chance said. "Don't you think she's been under there a long time?"

"She's a good swimmer," said Elise. "Well, a good dog paddler, anyway."

"She isn't swimming, she's floating," he pointed out.

"We absolutely have to pick the wedding colors," Phoebe said.

"You mean, *I* have to pick them!" said his sister.

"I'm getting a little concerned about your friend." Chance didn't want to overdramatize the situation by plunging into the pool fully clothed, but the woman's lungs must be near bursting.

"She's fine," Elise said. "Her hands are moving under the water. If she'd lost consciousness, she couldn't maintain a vertical position."

Chase knelt at the edge of the pool. The hair bobbed upward, then lowered again. The woman was deliberately staying down there, all right, but why was she behaving so bizarrely?

Phoebe joined Chance at the side of the pool. She was focused on Daisy, looking concerned. "Is she on medication?" he asked.

"Maybe hormones. I think she has what they used to call a female condition," said Phoebe, her face suddenly turning red. "Maybe I shouldn't have shared that with you. It just slipped out in my worry."

"Hormones don't make a person act like a lunatic. At least, I don't think so." Chance's own lungs were aching in sympathy. Unable to stand the suspense, he reached into the pool and grasped the woman's shoulders, getting his jacket cuffs and watch soaked in the process.

She had smooth shoulders, he noticed distractedly. Touching her bare skin gave him a slight tingle.

When he pulled, she shot to the surface, gasping and sputtering. Waterlogged hair clung to her cheeks, and for a disconnected moment he thought he was imagining the resemblance.

But it was her. Deirdre.

Daisy, he thought in confusion. Deirdre *was* Daisy. But why on earth had his sister's friend run away from him?

DAISY HADN'T MEANT to stay under the water so long. She'd gone down on an impulse and then, hearing the blurred echo of Chance's voice, had clung to her sanctuary single-mindedly.

She was glad he'd pulled her up. And humiliated at being discovered. If she hadn't been coughing so hard, she would have raced for the building before anyone could start asking questions, but her own frailty trapped her.

Clinging to Chance's strong arms, she leaned against the edge of the pool and sucked in deep, agonizing lungfuls of air. Only gradually did she realize the man's sleeves were drenched, not to mention that was obviously a very expensive watch.

Embarrassed, she eased her grip and moved away. "I'm sorry."

"Are you all right?" His deep tones echoed through her.

She nodded, keeping her eyes averted. Her friends were studying her with varying degrees of puzzlement.

"Is it the hormones?" Elise asked. "Are you having hot flashes?"

"No, of course not!" Could this get any more awkward? Daisy wondered.

The last thing she wanted was for Chance to hear about her medical condition. A guy like him would probably be repelled by the mention of endometriosis.

In fact, a playboy like him would head for the hills if he found out how badly she wanted a child. Especially if he learned that she needed to get pregnant soon to ease her condition and help prevent future infertility.

Daisy longed to hold a baby in her arms. It scared her that already there was a chance she couldn't conceive.

The gentle, understanding man that she dreamed of marrying would accept her without hesitation and stand by her no matter what. A man like Chance, on the other hand, was likely to wrinkle his nose and hightail it in pursuit of a woman with no imperfections attached.

Did he have to look so gorgeous, with the late-afternoon light bringing out the strength of his face and the deceptive sensitivity of his gray gaze? she wondered. It would have been hard to keep her distance, except for the fact that she could barely move.

"You wouldn't happen to be in need of mouth-to-mouth resuscitation, would you?" he teased, seeming unaware of the breeze that fluttered engagingly through his soft hair. Even the elements conspired on Chance's behalf.

"I'm a little cold." Getting out of the pool would feel even colder, but Daisy needed to escape the curious stares of her friends. Not to mention the ever-inquisitive Frannie Fitzgerald, who stood on her patio with hands on hips, watching them with interest.

"Which towel's yours?" When she pointed, Chance brought it from a nearby bench.

As she climbed from the water, he wrapped it around her, his hands lingering longer than strictly necessary. Despite her better judgment, she didn't mind.

"Honestly, we didn't realize anything was wrong," Phoebe said. "Should I call a doctor?"

"Nothing *is* wrong." Daisy wished her teeth would

stop chattering. "It's my own stupid fault. I had this impulse to see how long I could stay underwater."

"Why?" asked her friend.

"Because I'm an idiot," she said.

"You look kind of blue," Elise said. "I don't care for that shade. We can scratch it off our list for the wedding."

Daisy couldn't help chuckling at her friend's nonsense. Chance circled his arm more closely around her. He didn't seem to notice the water dripping onto his suit and shoes.

"I repeat, we need to try on dresses before we make a decision," said Phoebe.

"There is no 'we' making this decision," Elise said. "I'm consulting you two out of the goodness of my heart."

"Saturday," Phoebe said. "I'm free to shop in the afternoon."

Elise shrugged. "Okay by me." When Daisy coughed, her friend said, "I'll answer for her. She's taking a few hours off to join us."

"But I have a show opening that night."

"That's why you hired that assistant. Right?"

There was no denying it. "Right."

"I'm taking Daisy inside to dry off," Chance told them.

"I can go alone."

"No," he replied firmly. "You need me to look after you."

Daisy's heart twisted in a funny, scary, delicious way. She knew it was just Chance's suave charm coming into play, but she wished so hard that he meant it.

"Before you go," his sister said, "was there a reason you wanted to see me, big bro?"

"Nothing urgent. I'll catch you later," he said.

Daisy knew she shouldn't let him walk her to her condo. If she did, he might come inside. And if that happened, she might not be able to resist him any more than she had two months ago.

What power did this man have over her? Sternly she reminded herself that he possessed no power that she didn't grant him.

Yet, despite her resolve to the contrary, she let him escort her all the way to unit 2E.

AFTER SEEING SO MANY devastated marriages, Chance had set very high standards for the woman he would someday wed, and, since college, no one had come close to meeting them. Certainly he was better off not getting involved with someone as unpredictable as Deirdre.

Yet his feelings refused to yield to logic. Her mercurial quality made her all the more fascinating, and the way she nestled within the circle of his arm inspired a longing to protect her.

From his greater height, he studied Daisy's well-defined nose and thick lashes. Were her eyes really as green as he remembered? When she opened her condo and turned toward him, he saw that they were.

"Thanks," she said.

"That's it?" He couldn't believe she meant to leave him standing there.

"You want to dry your watch and make sure it works?" she asked.

"Of course it works. It's water resistant," he said. "That isn't the point. Either you're trying to duck the issue or you want to have a highly personal conversation right here in the hallway. Given the nosiness of your neighbors, I would advise against it.''

A panicky expression crossed her face. It made Chance feel like an ogre for twisting her arm, but darn it, he wasn't going to let Deirdre escape again. Whatever she was hiding needed to come out in the open.

At least now he knew she wasn't married. Or an escaped felon. Or any of the other unlikely possibilities that had occurred to him.

''Come on.'' He made the decision for her, escorting her inside and closing the door behind them. ''Let's get this over with.''

''That sounds…threatening.''

''Absolutely not,'' he said. ''I just want to clear the air.''

She took a deep breath. ''Okay,'' she said, then hesitated, as if thinking things over.

The condo surprised him, when Chance allowed himself to look around. Subconsciously he'd expected to find it flowery and old-fashioned, with a few stuffed animals or dolls tucked among ruffled pillows.

Instead it was subtle with a couple of key focal points. His attention fixed first on a red, orange and pink blanket woven in a jagged design, draped across the back of the off-white couch. Then he noticed, in an opposing corner, a large ceramic planter with a band of molten red against a multitextured blue-gray surface.

Everything else in the room flowed in muted colors and shapes. Chairs, lamps, draperies, all had been selected with a discerning taste.

''Who did your decorating?'' He wouldn't mind hiring the same designer to complete the interior of his house.

"I did." Nibbling at her lower lip, Daisy edged toward the kitchen. "Would you like coffee?"

"No, but help yourself, if it'll warm you," he said. "Better yet, get dressed."

"I'm not cold."

"I insist."

"Are you going to supervise to make sure I put on something warm enough?" Dismay at the implication made her eyes fly open. Definitely green.

"Would you like me to?" Chance hadn't expected the conversation to take such a flirtatious turn, but he didn't object. "After your antics at the pool, I'd say a little guidance wouldn't be amiss."

"Guidance?" She drew the towel tightly around herself. It failed to hide her slim legs or the graceful curve of her neck. "I'm not your little sister."

"I'm aware of that."

"Back off." Her toes curled inside her thong sandals. "I don't need anyone taking charge of me."

"All I want is information," he said. "Why did you bail out on me that night?"

"You know, on second thought you're right. I'd better put on warm clothes." Like a will-o'-the-wisp, she vanished into the bedroom, leaving Chance gritting his teeth in frustration.

DAISY STRUGGLED to peel the damp suit from her goose-bumpy flesh. It didn't help to know that the best-looking man she'd ever met was waiting in the next room and that, by all indications, she had only to summon him and he'd come to undress her, inch by quivering inch.

Undress her and how many other women in the next few days and nights?

She couldn't tear from her mind the image of him standing in the sunshine, holding that blond woman outside the restaurant. Gazing into her pouty face. Surrounding her with his strength, just as he'd done a few minutes ago to Daisy.

It was unfair that a man should possess such tenderness, such endearing manners—and such a complete lack of faithfulness.

Daisy wasn't usually a sucker for a ladies' man. She'd seen how her mother struggled to bring up a child alone, and her heart still bore the scars inflicted by an absentee father.

But there was something different about Chance Foster, a genuine quality that sneaked past her defenses. Should she be honest with him about why she'd left and risk letting him persuade her to try again?

Still debating, Daisy put on a long, hand-dyed dashiki her mother had made and went into the bathroom. She dragged a brush through her hair and stared at herself in the mirror.

Her skin looked more flushed than usual, probably from the sun, or could it be the result of her hormone pills? The doctor had changed her prescription a few months earlier, and she'd been suffering minor side effects.

The reminder of her medical condition threw cold water on temptation. A man like Chance Foster, attractive and successful and popular, would never have the patience to put up with her problems.

The doctor had said she might not be able to have a baby at all. The golden boy of Phoenix wasn't very likely to choose a wife who couldn't provide him with suitably golden offspring, was he? Even assuming, and it was a huge long shot, that he ever developed serious intentions toward Daisy.

Perhaps other women could afford to risk their hearts on him. She couldn't. She needed a kind and undemanding family man who was at no risk of dragging her emotions onto a roller coaster the way her father had done.

No matter how much she wanted to hold Chance Foster one more time, she couldn't afford to.

Squaring her shoulders, Daisy went to face him.

CHANCE COULDN'T FIGURE OUT why it took a woman so long to throw on a few clothes. On the other hand, he enjoyed knowing that Daisy cared enough about him to take pains with her appearance.

He appreciated women who groomed themselves well. And he knew a lot of them. Chance had heard that other men envied the way he showed up at charity and social events with one beauty after another.

What they didn't know was that most of the ladies were platonic friends. Few men took the time to listen or to share big brotherly advice, and he'd discovered that women were hungry for uncritical companionship.

He was no monk, of course. There'd been a few lovers during the ten years since he finished law school, when his fiancée broke off their engagement to pursue her dream of a high-powered career.

It was a dream Chance had once shared, but he was a realist about his circumstances. Most of the time, anyway.

He didn't regret that none of his later relationships had resulted in marriage. The women had been wrong for him, and not ready for marriage, either, in his view.

As a divorce attorney, he'd learned to identify the

danger signs. Unrealistic expectations. Financial irresponsibility. Unwillingness to discuss differences of opinion.

Chance had long ago discarded the romantic notion that love was the essential ingredient in marriage, because he'd seen how quickly it could fade under adversity. He knew the keys were mutual respect and compatibility, not head-over-heels passion.

At least he'd thought so until he met Deirdre. He couldn't explain what had hit him. Heaven knew he'd spent two months trying to talk himself out of his burning desire to see her again, without success.

With Deirdre he felt a new kind of connection. He wanted to linger in her arms, to listen to her breathing, to hear her laughter. When he'd awakened the morning after they'd made love and found her gone, the house had echoed with emptiness.

Chance was flipping through an art magazine, wondering if this was where she got her decorating ideas, when Daisy came out wearing an African-style dress whose soft fabric molded to the contours of her body. The dress was neither stylish nor glamorous, but on her, highly appealing.

"Feeling better?" he asked.

Her reddish-brown hair bobbed as she nodded. It reminded him of the woman he'd seen this afternoon.

"You don't happen to work at an art gallery, do you?" he said.

"I own one." Daisy led the way into the kitchen, where she poured herself coffee from a carafe and stuck it in the microwave to reheat. "Native Art, downtown."

"No wonder you did such a great job of selecting your furnishings." He made a mental note to visit her gallery. Often. "So you work one block from my office. I haven't been imagining things."

"You mean you saw that oddball woman ducking into alleys whenever you walked by?" Daisy shrugged. "That was me."

"Care to provide an explanation?" he said. "Or do you behave this way with all your lovers?"

She snatched the coffee mug from the microwave, and for a moment he feared she was going to throw it at him. "That was uncalled for."

"A low blow," he agreed. "I'm sorry. I'm also still awaiting your answer about why you left that night."

"I left because I don't think we're suited to each other," she said. "And I was embarrassed. It isn't my custom to go to bed with strangers."

"That doesn't explain why you couldn't wait until morning to tell me. I thought I'd done something to offend you. You owe me an apology and a lot better reason than you've given."

Chance knew he was pressuring her. Had she been a casual friend, he would have backed off and listened sympathetically. But he had no intention of behaving that way with Daisy.

She'd hurt him, and it was going to hurt him even more if he couldn't make her change her mind. He wanted more of the excitement that had been missing from his relationships since college. He wanted another chance with this woman.

Daisy sniffed at the coffee and set the cup down without tasting it. "You're right, it was cowardly. I'm sorry. You have every right to be angry. So I guess you don't want to see me again, and that's the end of it."

"Wrong," he said.

"You can't possibly expect—I mean, this is all mixed up. My coffee doesn't even smell appetizing. I must be really wired." She paced into the living room. "We should never have—done what we did. What would your sister say? And Phoebe?"

"I can't imagine why they should object," Chance returned.

"Oh, they won't. They'll fuss. They'll cheer us on. They'll shove us together at every possible opportunity," Daisy said. "They'll drive us both crazy."

"So you're rejecting me because I'm Elise's brother? And because my sister would approve of our getting involved? That doesn't make sense."

Daisy took a stance on the pale carpet. "I answered your question about why I left you. I knew we were wrong for each other, and I was embarrassed. That's the whole story."

Chance knew it couldn't be. His lawyer instincts prodded him to back her into a corner, argue until she broke down and win the case through logic. But if he did that, he would lose any hope of winning her heart.

Instead he said, "Maybe we could start over. You have no reason to be embarrassed now, because I'm not a stranger, and—"

"I didn't agree to a debate," she said. "This conversation is over."

"Are you asking me to go?"

"No hard feelings, but yes."

For one agonizing moment he held her gaze. She was so much smaller than he but equally strong willed. He'd met his match, he thought. Perhaps in more ways than one.

"I yield the point," he said. "And, Daisy?"

"Yes?"

"Please stop ducking around corners and nearly drowning yourself to avoid me," he said. "I'm not an ogre."

"I'll remember that," she said.

Judging by the glint in her eye, Chance knew she was teasing. He just hoped that behind the teasing lay an attraction to match his own.

Chapter Three

He certainly wasn't an ogre, Daisy thought as she closed the door behind him. He was sexy and bewitching and even a bit vulnerable.

If only she could yield to instinct and haul him into her bedroom. If only she had a heart of cast iron and could simply enjoy the moment.

But Chance had the power to hurt her badly. And eventually he'd do it, either through one big abandonment or through little betrayals over time.

In the meantime he was too forceful. Daisy had nearly backed down beneath his verbal onslaught, had nearly apologized and admitted she'd been wrong.

She didn't want to back down. She didn't want a man who could override her better judgment and control her actions.

In her adult life she'd been involved seriously with two men. They'd seemed different from each other on the surface, but underneath they'd been alike.

Commanding. Insistent. Wanting to take charge of her. In both cases, she'd broken things off after a nasty argument.

Maybe it was because she'd grown up without a father or even a grandfather, but in Daisy's experience it simply wasn't possible to negotiate with a man. There was no way to share power, only fight or flight.

She needed a low-key fellow who wouldn't lock horns with her. So why wasn't she attracted to a guy like that?

Daisy wandered into the kitchen and tried to concentrate on fixing dinner. She couldn't stop thinking about Chance. The lingering scent of his aftershave drifted from the living room, as if a part of him had permeated her condo.

While using the electric opener on a can of soup, she noticed a white paperback wedged between two cookbooks on the counter. What a relief to discover where she'd stuck it! She'd been afraid a deep-lying emotional reluctance had led her to lose the book her friends had bought her, *2001 Ways to Wed.*

The book worked, all right. Using it in an attempt to help Daisy, both Phoebe and Elise had fallen in love.

So far she hadn't done more than glance through it. But if it could help her find Mr. Right, she'd be able to put Chance Foster out of her mind once and for all.

Daisy opened the book. "Okay, Jane Jasmine," she said, as if the author were standing in front of her. "What pearls of wisdom do you have to offer me?"

Flipping through the pages, she noted and rejected some of the suggestions. She wasn't going to meet the man of her dreams at the workplace. Sean O'Reilly, her assistant at the gallery, was a kid of twenty-two, eight years younger than she was.

Nor was she likely to find the man of her dreams next door. She'd already ruled out the brother of her next-door neighbor, Elise. The condo on the other side belonged to a middle-aged married couple with school-age children.

Daisy stopped at a chapter entitled "If He Knew Me, He'd Hate Me—Or Would He?"

All of us fear rejection. And many of us secretly feel unworthy of love. Putting the two areas of anxiety together, we may believe that the object of our interest couldn't possibly love us as we really are.

So we pretend to be something we aren't, or we hide our real self deep inside. This is exactly the opposite of what we should do if we want to find true love.

We need to be frank and honest. We need to take the risk of showing our true self to the one we care about.

I'm not suggesting you test your loved one's devotion by dropping your dirty boots on her spotless floor or unloading a day's worth of frustration by yelling at him. That's not honesty, it's inconsideration.

But if you're watching his football games and haven't seen your favorite ice skaters in months, tell him what you like. Look for a way to satisfy both your needs. Don't hide your interests, your fears, your hopes. Sharing them can only create a stronger bond between the two of you.

Skeptical, Daisy stuck the book back into place. The author's advice made sense up to a point, but how could she tell a formidable man like Chance Foster that she had run away because she knew that sooner or later he would break her heart?

And, having seen him again, she was more certain of that than ever.

"WHAT WAS ALL THAT ABOUT?" Elise demanded when Chance popped into her condo.

His sister had changed into shorts and a sleeveless buttoned shirt. With her medium-length brown hair clipped back, she looked too young to be a college professor. It was hard sometimes to remember that she was thirty-three and had a Ph.D.

"What was all what about?" he temporized. It had become a habit, as an attorney, to reveal as little as possible while he organized his thoughts.

Plus, Chance felt a natural restraint about revealing his emotions. Perhaps it came from being a big brother and taking a lot of responsibility for his sisters. He'd seen the pressure that having eight children put on his parents and had done his best to spare them from unnecessary worry.

In any case, he didn't like having other people see his vulnerabilities. Not even Elise.

"I got the notion you and Daisy had met before." She turned her back and marched into the kitchen. Judging by the onions, mushrooms, eggs and cheese on the counter, she was planning to cook an omelette. "You're going to have to satisfy my curiosity if you expect me to fix you dinner."

"I had no such expectation," he said, although the sight of the ingredients made his mouth water. "And naturally, I wouldn't dream of preparing one of my kitchen-sink salads unless you answer a few questions I happen to have."

Chance was famous in the Foster household for salads in which, according to his sisters, he tossed everything but the kitchen sink. Starting with a base of greens and tomatoes, he would hunt through the pantry and come up with sardines or tuna, water chestnuts, cashew nuts, crispy Chinese noodles, garbanzo beans or whatever else was on hand.

Elise cracked a couple of eggs into a bowl and regarded him assessingly. "Well, all right. I'll bet I can tell plenty about you and Daisy from whatever questions you ask, anyway."

"You should have been a lawyer."

"Spare me!" she cried in mock horror. "Two in one family?" She cracked a couple more eggs into the bowl. Elise would never put that many eggs in an omelette unless she was expecting company, Chance noted happily.

"By the way, I came over here to talk to you about your wedding plans," he said. "As an attorney..."

"If you say one word about James and me needing a prenuptial agreement, I'll wring your neck!" She chopped the onions hard against the cutting board.

From the refrigerator, Chance fetched the salad's basic ingredients. "If I were *his* lawyer, seeing how wealthy he is, I'd insist on it. As your brother, however, I'm delighted that he hasn't asked for one."

Elise's mouth twitched. She was only slightly mollified, he could tell. "Then what did you want to say?"

"That I hope you've taken my advice about getting premarital counseling." Opening the cupboard, he stared at the rows of cans before selecting artichoke hearts and pinto beans. Chopped mild chili peppers. Sliced black olives. And a bag of sunflower seeds.

"We don't need it." His sister splashed olive oil into her omelette pan. "We love each other and we're already on the same wave length."

"How do you plan to handle finances?" Chance challenged. "Which relatives will you spend Christmas with? How many children do you want? What if you get a once-in-a-lifetime offer to teach at a foreign university?''

"We'll deal with those issues as they come up." Elise's thoughtful expression indicated he'd hit home, however.

"It's better if you discuss potential areas of conflict before there's an urgent need," Chance informed her.

His sister released an exasperated breath. "Don't you ever stop being bossy?"

"Will I ever stop caring about you? No." He drained the salad ingredients and tossed them together.

Elise didn't say any more as she concentrated on pouring the mixture into the pan, letting it cook and deftly folding it. A few minutes later the two of them sat at the table, sharing their creations.

"Tell me about you and Daisy," she said.

There was no point in playing coy. "I met her at your engagement party."

She stopped, a forkful of salad halfway to her mouth. "Daisy is Deirdre? I don't believe it!"

He thanked his innate reserve for the fact that he hadn't told about taking Deirdre home with him. He'd said only that he'd met a charming woman and wondered if anyone knew her phone number. "To make matters worse, I told her my name was Charles. So she didn't know who I was, either."

"And you like each other? How perfect!" Elise crowed. "Phoebe and I have been trying to find a guy for Daisy for months!"

"So you've told me," Chance said. "I don't understand why. An attractive woman like her should have men swarming around."

"She's picky," his sister said. "We've been trying to find the *right* man."

"So she's hard to please." He poured a little more vinegar and oil on his salad. "Does that mean she's unreliable? Does she change her mind often?"

"There's a difference between being discerning and being capricious." Now Elise sounded like the professor she was instead of like his kid sister. "There's nothing flighty about Daisy."

Chance hesitated. There was another thing he wanted to know that might shed light on Daisy's behavior. It was highly personal, though. "Phoebe mentioned a female condition. I don't know much about these things."

Elise set down her fork. "I don't know if I should tell you."

"Then don't."

Elise stared out the window, considering. "I don't think Daisy would mind if I explained her condition to you. I've heard her tell others about it, people who aren't that close to her. I think she's actually trying to educate people about the condition.

"She has endometriosis. The way Daisy explained it, tissue that's supposed to be lining the uterus appears in other parts of the body. It can be minor or really nasty. Her case is kind of in the middle but getting worse. It can make it hard to have a baby, so if she wants one, she needs to have it soon."

The possibility that Daisy's life might be in danger sent an icy wave of fear flooding through Chance. "It isn't like cancer, is it?"

"No, no!" His sister patted his hand. "The way she explained it, it's as if a bit of your heart tissue landed in your elbow."

"Excuse me?"

"It would beat, just like it always does, so you'd

have this weird pulsing elbow. So this female tissue, well, it behaves normally, only it's in the wrong place. That can cause a lot of pain. Especially once a month.''

"I get the picture," he said.

Chance wasn't sure whether Daisy's endometriosis had anything to do with her decision to flee from his house and avoid him afterward. It certainly introduced a complication that would affect any man she married. But a guy worth his salt married for better or for worse, in sickness and in health.

Wait a minute. Why was he thinking about Daisy in connection with marriage?

They weren't even dating, let alone close to becoming engaged. In fact, she'd just thrown him out of her apartment.

Elise regarded him shrewdly. "So have I put you off my friend?" she asked.

"You mean because she has this condition?" he said. "No."

"I probably shouldn't have said anything." She stood up and carted her dishes to the counter. "Me and my big mouth."

"I'm your brother."

"Yeah, but she likes you."

"You think so?" The observation lifted his spirits.

"I've seen Daisy around a lot of guys," Elise said. "You're different. It wasn't anything she said or did, exactly. It was that, well, I could tell she was aware of you every second."

He waited, hoping for more concrete details of the way she'd looked at him, or a comment she'd made after the party.

"You're doing the dishes, right?" said his sister,

seemingly unaware of his hunger for more details about the elusive Daisy.

ALL FRIDAY MORNING Daisy's stomach churned. At first she thought she might be coming down with a virus, but toward lunchtime she got hungry.

It wasn't the first time she'd felt queasy since the doctor changed her medication. It hadn't helped that, lacking medical insurance because she was self-employed, Daisy had allowed a few weeks to elapse while she waited to have her new prescription filled through a cheap mail-order pharmacy.

Going on and off medication must have played havoc with her hormones. Yet she couldn't justify the cost of another doctor visit when she felt certain the situation would resolve itself as her system adjusted.

"You feeling better?" asked her assistant, Sean, as he carted a collage from Gallery III into the back room. They had to take down one exhibit and put up the new one today.

"Yes. In fact, I'm starving," she admitted. "Is that the last piece?"

"All done," he confirmed.

Daisy stepped into the bare-walled gallery. She'd been visualizing the new exhibit ever since she'd arranged for the one-woman show months ago. It would be the artist's first major exhibit in the United States, and invitations to Saturday night's wine and cheese opening had been mailed last week.

Shakira Benjamin was a gifted African-American painter and teacher who'd had a studio in Germany before relocating to Mesa, near Phoenix, about a year ago. Daisy felt lucky to have her affiliated with the gallery.

"What now?" asked Sean, joining her. A recent college graduate, he wore his blond hair long and unstyled, hanging over the shoulders of a blue workshirt.

As usual, bits of sawdust clung to his jeans. The loft where he lived and worked on his wood sculptures was no doubt coated with the stuff.

"We'll need to put these up." She indicated a pile of rough-textured cloths in the three primary colors.

The artist's acrylic paintings placed superrealistic images of people on impressionistic backgrounds, in sepia or black-and-white tones reminiscent of old photographs. The overall effect would be harsh without offsetting color on the walls.

Daisy's favorite was a painting of two Native American children, one in traditional buckskin and the other in modern clothes, playing a game that resembled jacks. The blurry background might be viewed as either a cluster of ancient multilevel pueblos or as a modern cityscape.

"Okay, where do you want me to hang this?" Sean picked up a yellow burlap rectangle.

"I'll show you." Daisy fetched a folding ladder and placed it against the back wall. As she climbed, a momentary light-headedness made her halt. "Wow. I must be hungrier than I thought."

"Do you want me to make a sandwich run?"

"In a minute." After descending, she handed Sean a sketch she'd made, showing how the rectangles should be draped to complement the paintings. "Think you can handle it?"

"Sure." His can-do attitude, which she'd appreciated when he first came here as a student intern, was the reason she'd hired him. Working alongside him, she had learned she could rely on his excellent artistic judgment.

"We probably won't be able to finish mounting everything and adjusting the lights till tomorrow." Daisy hoped the light-headedness was only a temporary phenomenon, because it was going to be a busy day. "I've got a commitment in the afternoon for a few hours, so we'll have to do it early."

"Okay by me."

She didn't mind that Elise and Phoebe had more or less coerced her into going shopping with them on Saturday afternoon. All the same, she hoped they found dresses quickly.

Bells jingled as the front door opened. Daisy brushed lint off her ivory blouse and calf-length, striped tan and blue skirt—one of her mother's creations—and went to check on the visitor.

Bright daylight silhouetted Chance Foster's well-built frame. Even when the door closed, the glare faded slowly, and it was a moment before she realized he was carrying a pizza and a carton of drinks.

His self-possessed stance and the welcoming indentation in his cheek couldn't hide the hunger in his gaze. How could a man look so pleasantly accommodating and so virile at the same time?

"I hope you haven't eaten," he said.

Before Daisy could reply, Sean appeared at her elbow. "Wow!" he said. "You sent out?" Then he noticed Chance's tailored suit. "Must be some snazzy restaurant if their delivery guys dress like this!"

"We aim to please." Chance set the pizza and drinks on a low front table that held informational pamphlets. "Chance Foster. I'm a friend of Daisy's." Sean introduced himself, and the two men shook hands.

It would be rude to reject his offering of food after he'd gone to so much trouble, Daisy told herself. Besides, the scents of cheese and spices were enough to overpower even the most iron will. "Thanks," she said.

"It's Mexican-style pizza." Chance cleared the pamphlets aside while Sean fetched folding chairs. Ordinarily Daisy ate in the back room, but it would be cramped for the three of them, so she didn't protest.

A middle-aged couple wandered into the gallery. They smiled at the lunchtime tableau and began browsing through the Gallery I exhibit of beaded jewelry and headdresses.

The hot sausage and chili peppers on the pizza gave Daisy a moment's pause. She was too hungry to resist, however, and found that they didn't upset her stomach as much as she'd feared.

"I work a block away," Chance explained to Sean. "I'm a family law attorney."

"So how do you two know each other?" the young man asked guilelessly.

"His sister…"

"…lives next door…"

"…ran into each other…"

"…engagement party."

They finished at the same time. Sean regarded them with a puzzled expression. "I see."

"Actually, my interest in Daisy is partly professional." Chance managed to eat his pizza without getting cheese on his chin, a trick that Sean hadn't mastered, Daisy noted.

"She needs a lawyer?" the young man asked.

"Not my profession. Hers." Chance handed around

cups of soft drinks. "I need artwork for my house and I could use her expert advice."

Daisy hoped he wasn't suggesting that she visit his house again. She also hoped this wasn't a ploy to get her back into his bed. "I could show you our portfolio of artists."

The middle-aged couple stopped nearby. "Can I help you?" Daisy asked. When they nodded, Sean went to assist them in trying on jewelry.

"I need more than a few items." Chance spoke coolly, in a low voice. "I'm a strong believer in seeing the big picture, and when it comes to art, I lack your ability to visualize a room in advance."

Daisy took a deep breath. "From what I've seen of your house..."

"You'll need to take another look. In daylight." He wasn't asking, she realized. Chance had made his decision and expected her to go along with it.

"But..."

"I want the whole effect carefully thought out. It's going to involve getting a few items of new furniture, too, and repainting if necessary. I realize you're not an interior designer, but the sculpture and paintings will be the focus."

Daisy wanted to refuse. She didn't like being railroaded, and she didn't want to venture into Chance Foster's house again.

Sitting across from him in her gallery, despite the nearness of Sean and the customers, her whole body sparkled with the man's energy. The restraint in his gray eyes and elegant suit only emphasized the contours of his body and the potent sexuality she remembered all too vividly.

She wasn't sure she could stay out of Chance's bed. Alone in his house…

"We're talking about a large expenditure," he went on. "When I bought the house, I budgeted a considerable sum for art. It's time I spent it."

Unfair! she wanted to cry. Even a successful gallery like Native Art operated on a thin profit margin. She couldn't afford to pass up this opportunity. Besides, Daisy owed it to her artists to do her best for them.

And, she recalled, that night when she entered his house, he'd apologized for the sparse furnishings and mentioned that one of these days he was going to buy paintings. So he wasn't simply manipulating her.

She assumed an impersonal tone. "I represent dozens of artists. I'm sure we can find special pieces for you."

The couple made a purchase and left, and Sean rejoined them. "What did I miss?"

"Miss Redford is going to take a look at my house this afternoon and make recommendations." Chance wiped his hands on a napkin and stood up. "I leave work early on Fridays. Pick you up around three, all right? Nice to meet you, Sean." With a friendly nod, he departed.

Daisy sat motionless, stunned. She hadn't agreed to go to his house so soon, or to ride with him, either.

"Seems like a nice guy." Sean took another bite of pizza. "Hey, don't worry. Using your outline, I can get the show mounted by myself. Fridays are always slow anyway."

"Let's see how much progress we can make before three o'clock," she said.

Daisy knew when she'd been outmaneuvered. Well, she could hold her own with Chance Foster and she was going to prove it to him.

Chapter Four

Chance hadn't intended to corral Daisy into touring his house that afternoon. He'd gone by her gallery in a polite attempt to reestablish a friendly relationship and to ask for a professional consultation.

Something about the woman brought out the bossy side of him, he admitted as he finished making notes for a custody brief to write over the weekend.

Maybe it was the way she never gave an inch. And why did she have to employ a peppy young assistant who hovered over her adoringly?

She'd looked so cute in that demure long skirt, with a strand of auburn hair clinging to one cheek. And so surprised to see him, as if she weren't sure how to react. Chance had instinctively seized the advantage.

He wished he knew what it was about her that he found so captivating. It seemed unlikely she would fit his standards for the ideal wife, in light of the way she'd run from him and then refused to give a credible explanation.

Reliability and communication. Those were two musts that he would include if he ever wrote *A Lawyer's Guide to Making Matrimony Work*.

Probably no one would buy it, though, even if he

did. In his observation, people were irrational when it came to marriage.

Chance copied his notes from the computer's hard drive onto a diskette and dropped it in his briefcase. At his home office, he kept a library of legal references on CD-ROM, so he didn't have to cart heavy books home.

It was a quarter to three, which meant that, if he left now, he should arrive at the gallery right on the hour. Perfect timing suited Chance.

In his front office he found Nell Beecham closing the books for the week. The secretary whipped around to regard him sternly.

"Leaving fifteen minutes early, Mr. Foster?" she asked. At sixty-seven, Nell brought nearly a half century of experience to the job, along with strong opinions about how people ought to behave. Including her boss.

"I'm picking someone up at three," he said.

Her frown mutated into an approving half smile. "Good. You'll be on time." If he thought he'd passed inspection, however, Chance had congratulated himself too soon. "I don't recall setting up an appointment for you."

When he'd hired Nell, one of his friends had warned that he would be getting a mother figure in the office. Chance didn't mind.

For one thing, top-notch secretaries were hard to find. For another, as the oldest of eight children, he'd filled the role of a quasiadult for so long that he was on more or less equal terms with his own parents, so he figured he could handle an office mother as well.

"It's the owner of the Native Art gallery," he told her. "I'm consulting her about my house."

"Some of the objects they display are a bit odd," she said. "I'm not a fan of modern art myself. However, they have an excellent reputation."

"I'll be the one who makes the final decisions," he assured her. "Have a lovely weekend."

"Don't forget you're due in court Monday morning," she said.

"I won't." He didn't have to remind her about locking up and depositing the week's checks. Nell Beecham was as reliable as a bank president.

She kept her private life to herself, though. Although she'd mentioned her grown children, the only pictures on her desk were of her two Siamese cats.

He wondered what she did in her spare time. A woman as energetic and organized as Nell wouldn't likely sit around knitting cat booties. Still, he didn't intend to get nosy.

Traffic was heavy, Chance found when his sports car exited the parking garage, but he didn't mind. He liked working in a high-rise, metropolitan area with easy access to suburbs.

In recent years Phoenix had become a haven for the winter weary, and while the migration was good for business, it resulted in L.A.-style jams. The inconvenience was worth the price, in his opinion.

Still, he didn't have the big-city career he'd once aspired to. Although Phoenix was thriving, it couldn't compare in significance to New York or the nation's capital.

Sometimes Chance felt a stirring of regret at not having pushed harder to follow in his former fiancée Gillian's footsteps. The last he'd heard, she'd made junior partner at her Washington, D.C. law firm and was handling a high-profile case against the government.

The thought of bringing his skills to a case like that gave Chance a jolt of adrenaline. It would be a great feeling, a rush almost like sex.

He double-parked in front of Native Art and was wondering whether to dash inside or go around through the alley when Daisy swung out with a farewell wave to someone inside. The youthful, devoted Sean O'Reilly, no doubt. If the young man ever quit, Chance wondered if Nell Beecham had a contemporary she could recommend as a replacement.

Daisy slid into the low passenger seat. The slit in her long skirt bared one shapely leg, until she tugged it into place and dropped a portfolio in her lap.

Clover, he thought. Or honey, that was what she smelled like.

"Busy afternoon?" he asked.

"We had to lug a bunch of paintings around," Daisy said. "We have an exhibit opening tomorrow night."

He recalled seeing a poster inside the gallery. "Shakira Benjamin, right?"

"Yes. Some of her work might suit you," Daisy said. "You're welcome to stop by. We'll have wine and cheese, and our regular clients are interesting people."

She sounded all business. Chance respected professionalism in a woman. But he wished the invitation were for something a little more personal.

Daisy stared out her window as the flat, grid-pattern streets of the city flew by and they eased into the suburbs. She made no attempt at idle conversation.

Chance remembered what Elise had said about Daisy's medical condition. He hoped she wasn't in pain.

A man wanted to protect people he cared about. Especially women, and especially one as open-spirited and vulnerable as Daisy. He was particularly sympathetic to her fears about infertility.

Kids were precious. Chance didn't have a strong urge to become a father anytime soon, but he treasured the future possibility.

Of course, Daisy and the man she married could adopt children if she were unable to conceive. In the adoption cases Chance had handled, he'd been impressed by how quickly love and bonding occurred.

Startled, he realized that he'd once again associated Daisy with marriage. Was there such a thing as a male biological clock?

This whole attraction might be a simple matter of timing. But he doubted it.

Twenty minutes later they reached the suburb where he lived. Custom designed on a large lot secluded by low walls, the home had been on the market a year ago and he'd had to outbid two other would-be purchasers.

They passed through the gate and followed the curving driveway between low granite boulders and clumps of desert vegetation. The low-lying house might have sprung up by itself, so naturally did its red-tiled roof and salmon stucco walls fit into the landscape.

"It looks different in daylight," Daisy said. "I didn't realize how well the colors blended with the desert."

"I've had the landscaping updated around the front and in the courtyard." Chance parked beneath a carport. "The previous owner had tropical tastes that wasted a lot of water."

"I see what you mean about putting everything into a larger picture." Daisy scampered out of the car while he was still unfolding his long legs.

He caught up with her in front of the house and they strolled past relaxed plantings of golden yarrow and white blackfoot daisies. Loose material crunched underfoot. One of the first things Chance had done was to tear out the stark sidewalk and replace it with a naturalistic path of crumbly decomposed granite.

"You could use a bit of height out here," Daisy said. "I know several sculptors whose work would fit right in. In fact, we've got an exhibit in one of our galleries that might appeal to you."

"I'll take a look during the opening tomorrow."

He unlocked the wide door and they stepped into the tile entryway, off which opened an expansive sunken living room. Beyond it, vertical blinds gave a striped glimpse of a walled rear courtyard.

"You've got a great setting for a sculpture garden," Daisy said. "This could be a real showplace. I presume that's what you have in mind?"

"Absolutely." At least, it *had* been in his mind— until she walked into his home.

Now Chance found it difficult to concentrate on anything except her scintillating presence and the memory of a night two months ago when they'd made love, starting right here in the front room.

He forced himself to pay attention to Daisy's insights about his home as they walked through the airy rooms. From time to time Daisy stopped to open her portfolio and show him photos of artists' work. Paintings, weavings, sculpture, ceramics.

She understood the effect he wanted and was able to articulate it in a way Chance couldn't, because he lacked the vocabulary of color and texture. She also noted where a love seat, small table or other furniture would fit into the scheme.

"If you want custom furniture, I know craftsmen who can make it for you," she said.

"I'm impressed. Did you always have an instinct for art, or did you have to study?"

"Both." Now that they'd completed their circuit, Daisy lowered the portfolio onto a table. They were standing where the family room joined the kitchen. "I studied design and ceramics at community college, but I've always been around artists. My mother designs and makes costumes. She dyes her own fabrics, too."

"Let's take a look at the rest of that portfolio," he said, and pulled a chair out, offering it to Daisy.

Her cheeks flushing with enthusiasm, Daisy flipped open the heavy book. Beneath clear plastic sheets, the photographs showed artists, their studios and a sampling of available pieces.

Many of the sculptors, Chance learned, were willing to create a piece on commission to fit the scale of a space or environment. He would be able to approve preliminary sketches and models.

Collecting art wasn't as simple as walking into a store and making his selections, he realized. It was far more exciting and personal.

Daisy lived and breathed art and understood her business. Chance would have been grateful to find her even if she didn't make his heart beat faster.

But despite his interest in the portfolio, he had a hard time not focusing on the fullness of her lips as she spoke. And on the swell of her breasts beneath the ivory blouse, close to where his hand rested on the table.

Daisy's presence and the lingering June sunlight made him forget the time, until his stomach reminded him. It was, Chance saw by his watch, nearly six o'clock.

"I'll contact the artists," he said. They'd decided on half a dozen people whose visions suited his taste.

"Just let me know what you order so I can follow up. Some artists have a tendency to get distracted," Daisy said. "I'll handle the billing, as well."

"Of course." It was time to take her home, but he didn't want to. "How about dinner? I've got salmon steaks we could grill, and I'll make one of my famous salads. Did Elise tell you about them?"

She shook her head. "I'm intrigued. But you don't have to feed me, especially not twice in one day."

"I've got to eat, too," he said. "And I prefer company."

Apparently he'd hit the right offhand tone, because she smiled instead of beating a retreat. "What can I fix?"

"How are you at microwaving baked beans?" he asked. "That's what I had in mind for a side dish."

Daisy flexed her forefinger. "I work out on the microwave daily."

Chance took her hand on the pretense of examining her finger muscles. It felt warm and dry and small in his big one. "You're in prime shape, I can see."

"Speaking of prime shape..." Her gaze lingered on the white shirt clinging to his chest. He'd removed his jacket and tie earlier, relieved to be free of the constraints. "I didn't see a home gym, but you must work out."

"I wear weights while I jog every morning," he said. "And I've got a routine of push-ups and sit-ups. You don't need special equipment for that."

She tore her attention away. A pinkish tone to her cheeks indicated she realized she'd been staring at him.

Chance's body responded with an infusion of heat and tension. It seemed so artificial, this gulf between them, when they were already lovers. Yet anything he said or did to change the situation was likely to spook her.

"Let's start cooking," he said. "I'm starved."

"You and me both."

They worked together, companionably. Instead of asking where things were kept, Daisy examined his drawers and cabinets for herself until she found the can of Boston beans, a microwave-safe casserole and a serving spoon. Chance liked her initiative.

While he grilled the salmon in the courtyard, he reflected that he hadn't cooked with a woman other than one of his sisters since he'd moved into this house. He'd had a few girlfriends at his previous place, a tract home, but had found it awkward trying to cook as they peppered him with queries.

The food tasted delicious, and for once Daisy didn't give the impression of trying to edge away from him. As they talked, she wore the same rapt expression as on their first night.

"I'm amazed at how much you've accomplished. Buying this house, for instance," she said. "Elise told me you put yourself through law school and helped pay for your younger sisters' education as well. It can't have been easy."

No, it hadn't been. "I didn't mind the long hours," Chance said. "And, as you can see, I've come out well enough. There's only one thing I regret."

"What's that?"

He'd never admitted this to anyone before. "I

wanted to get top grades and make the law review, but I couldn't quite manage it while working so many hours. That bothered me for quite a while."

"What if you had made the law review?" Daisy asked. "How would your life be different?"

No wasted sympathy, no superficial reassurances that it didn't matter. She'd cut right to the heart of the matter.

"I'd probably be in Washington or New York right now, handling cases on which the future of a company or an industry was riding," he said. "That's what my former fiancée is doing."

She finished a forkful of salmon before asking, "Is that what you really wish you were doing?"

Chance leaned back in his chair. "I envy Gillian sometimes. Remember the Robert Frost poem about two paths diverging in a yellow wood, and how he could have taken either one?"

Daisy nodded. "We read it in school."

"Sometimes I think it's still there, that fork in the road, that path I might have taken," he admitted.

"Are you tempted to go back and take the other path?"

He supposed he was, but high-stakes careers didn't land in a man's lap. "The opportunity will never arise unless I fight for it," he said. "And I'm too comfortable to do that."

Right now, for instance, it was a pleasure simply to sit opposite Daisy and watch emotions play across her expressive features. He couldn't imagine anywhere else he would rather be.

She was harder to categorize than any woman he'd ever known. Not aggressive—sometimes downright elusive—but highly competent. Sweet in a way he rarely encountered, yet possessing a quick mind. Sensual without flaunting it.

"Stay there and relax." He dragged himself from the cane-bottomed chair. "I'll clear."

"I'm helping." She popped up. "Otherwise you'll make me wash the dishes next time when there might actually *be* dishes." Taking a couple of serving dishes, Daisy marched into the kitchen.

Next time. Chance tried not to show how glad he was that she'd left that possibility open.

He hoped she wasn't in a hurry to leave. Their second evening together might not be as explosive as the first, but there was a lot to be said for slow-building fires.

THE SOFTNESS OF the light, the smoky scent of desert plants and Chance's easy presence made this house much too inviting. Why on earth had she stayed for dinner? Daisy asked herself, shoving a couple of paper plates into the wastebasket with unnecessary vigor.

She didn't understand what he wanted from her. He'd already made the conquest, hadn't he, so why seek a repeat performance? She certainly wasn't the glamorous type he usually sported on his arm.

If only she weren't so aware of him physically, the two of them might become friends. He was, after all, highly intelligent and intriguing.

While rinsing glasses in the sink, Daisy thought over their conversation. Elise hadn't mentioned Chance's former engagement. It added an unsuspected dimension to his character.

And, she reflected, it surprised her to learn that he had mixed feelings about the direction his career had taken. She couldn't imagine anything she would enjoy more than owning an art gallery, although she would like to earn more recognition for her pottery.

Chance moved behind her, carrying leftovers to the refrigerator, and Daisy's skin registered his heat even though they didn't touch. It took all her force of will to remain facing the sink.

"Did you enjoy the salad?" His voice sounded close to her ear. "I make it differently every time."

"The fresh chives were terrific," she said. "Did you grow them yourself?"

She made the mistake of turning around. He towered over her, inches away. She couldn't back up because she was standing against the counter.

"I grow herbs on the patio." Chance's voice was hypnotic, his eyes probing. "In pots, so I can move them into the shade if it gets too hot. Or indoors if it freezes." Frosts in Phoenix were usually brief. By contrast, summer highs often rose over 105 degrees.

The temperature in this room right now must be at least 110, Daisy thought wildly. If Chance touched her, she might burst into flames.

His hands rested lightly on her upper arms. "You're so intense. I can see everything you're feeling."

It was arrogant of the man to assume he could read her mind. Except that at the moment he probably could.

"We shouldn't..." He was so close, she could almost taste him. Wanted to taste him. Longed to taste him.

His lips brushed hers. Lightly, slowly. His nose grazed her cheek and he inhaled, drinking her in.

Mesmerized, Daisy yielded to the urging of her senses. She touched Chance's hair and relished the thickness of it. Nuzzled his throat, savoring the fragrance of his aftershave. Wound her arms around his neck and tipped her face to his.

His tongue flicked against hers and they met at fiery points along their bodies. Her erect nipples pressed into his chest. With one hand, he cupped her bottom and held her tight to his arousal.

Buds of excitement sprouted inside Daisy. She could hardly wait to strip away his clothes and rub her bare skin against his. To let him inside her, as she'd done before.

"I thought you'd hold out a lot longer," he teased, the vibrations of his voice shivering down her spine. "It's been much too long, Deirdre."

I thought you'd hold out... The words lingered in her mind. Was that what she presented, a challenge?

Maybe one conquest wasn't enough. Maybe Chance Foster wanted to prove that he could win her again.

Then what? Daisy wondered. Would he expect her to share him with that blonde and other women? Or would Chance, along with his pretext of hiring her artists, simply vanish like desert smoke?

Her yearning for him chilled. It was hard to extricate herself, but she ducked under his arm and twisted away.

"Did I say something wrong?" A last ray of sunlight through the window turned Chance's brown hair to molten gold.

"I...didn't mean to go this far," Daisy stammered. "I'm sorry."

"Aren't we a little old for coyness?" He raised one eyebrow, daring her to come back.

"I'll tell you what," she said. "I won't call a cab and sneak off. I'll let you drive me to the gallery."

Disappointment hovered in his eyes. Daisy clenched

her hands and held firm to her resolve. Rebelliously her lips continued to hum with the remembered pressure of his mouth. Her nipples were still hard, a state that almost certainly showed through her bra and the thin fabric of her blouse.

She wondered how he saw her. As a desirable object? As a toy to use and discard? All the pleasurable moments they'd shared tonight, fixing dinner, talking and laughing, were recast as empty manipulations.

Making no move to advance on her, Chance stood breathing raggedly. She wished she could tell whether he was angry.

At last he said, "Let me keep the portfolio another day. I want to study it."

To find an excuse to back out of buying artwork from her, she supposed. "Fine. You can drop it off Monday."

"Are you rescinding your invitation to the opening tomorrow night?" he asked.

"No." She'd forgotten about that. But why would he want to come?

"I'll bring it then." Chance lifted his jacket from the back of a chair and shrugged it on. "Let's get going...if you're sure you want to leave."

"Yes." Daisy scurried toward the front of the house. Her emotions swirled, so confused that she could hardly sort them out.

One thing was certain: he would never invite her to this house again.

THE EVENING BREEZE stung Chance's lips where, only minutes before, he'd been kissing Daisy. He still couldn't believe she'd shifted moods so suddenly and that he was taking her home.

He tried to remember what he'd said right before she withdrew, but nothing came to mind. Nothing significant, anyway. He'd been telling her that he missed her. What was wrong with that?

One thing he knew: clearly, this woman had been wounded. But not by him.

He'd made a mistake, rushing her. She needed time to learn to trust him.

Not only did Chance plan to commission plenty of artwork, he was going to require frequent consultations with her. Whether Daisy liked it or not, they were going to spend a lot of time in each other's company.

Chapter Five

On the drive back to the gallery, Daisy kept her window rolled down. Despite the rapidly dropping temperature outside, her internal heater was working full blast.

How unfair that Chance's nearness affected her this way! She was attuned to him, aware whenever he shifted gears or angled to check the side-view mirror. And she was lonely for his arms around her and impatient with her own longing.

She wouldn't bet five cents on the odds of his showing up at the opening tomorrow night. Most likely he would send a messenger with the portfolio on Monday, and that would be the last she'd hear from him.

He was so engaging, he'd nearly made it past her defenses. Mr. Charm, Elise kiddingly called her brother. In the darkness Daisy blushed to think how ridiculous she would look if her friend found out how easily she'd succumbed to him the first time, and how close she'd come to making the same mistake again.

From now on she expected nothing but a cold shoulder. That's the way Tony, her first serious boyfriend, had behaved after their big fight.

Clearly, Tony had felt she'd gone overboard when

she finally found the nerve to object to his domineering manner and frequent absences. The quarrel had degenerated into name-calling. Afterward, she'd made an attempt to patch things up, but he'd taken pride in being harsh and unforgiving.

She didn't suspect Chance of such childishness. If they ran into each other again, she expected polite, correct distance. And was prepared for the painful sight of a beautiful woman on his arm.

"I wish you'd tell me what flipped your switch," Chance said as they neared downtown. "If I did something to offend you, I'm sorry. It wasn't intentional."

"I'm not offended." Daisy was determined not to initiate any further quarrel. "My own behavior hasn't exactly been perfect."

"Was it my cooking?" he went on in a conversational tone. "I know I forgot dessert. We could stop for ice cream."

Daisy nearly laughed, the remark was so unexpected. "Your cooking was great." Oddly, she realized that the chalky feeling in her stomach had returned even though she'd eaten. Ice cream *would* help, but she shouldn't spend more time with Chance. "I'll pass on dessert, but thanks."

"I can understand that you might not want to get too friendly with a client," he went on. "But I was hoping in this case you would make an exception."

"That isn't it." Daisy hoped he wasn't going to keep probing for an explanation. It was embarrassing to admit that she knew she'd been duped. Besides, of course he would deny regarding her as a conquest.

For one tiny, hopeful second, she wondered if she might be wrong. Maybe this devastatingly handsome, successful playboy had fallen head over heels for an illegitimate girl who'd grown up barely above the poverty level. Who'd worked her way through community college, who made pottery she didn't dare display and who had a tendency to freckle.

Maybe he was tired of brilliant, ambitious, beautiful women like the one he'd nearly married.

Right.

They reached the gallery. "Where are you parked?" Chance asked.

"In back."

He drove around to the alley. There sat Daisy's aging station wagon, wedged into her reserved parking space. "Want me to follow you home?" he asked. "To make sure you get there safely?"

"My car may be old but I keep it in good repair," she replied.

"That wasn't what I meant." He draped one arm over her seat back, almost touching her. "I've got sisters, remember? It's a gentleman's job to see you home."

"This was business," Daisy reminded him.

"And pleasure." In the faint glow of a streetlamp, his rueful smile glistened. "For me, anyway."

She opened the door. "I'll be fine."

"I'll wait till you get it started."

As a businesswoman, Daisy often worked late and went home alone. Still, it was dark in this alley despite the streetlamp. His silent presence reassured her more than she cared to admit.

The station wagon started instantly. Chance followed until she emerged from the alley, then the sports car turned and shot off into the night.

Daisy drove past open nightclubs and restaurants.

People filled the sidewalks, chatting and laughing as they welcomed the beginning of the weekend.

She wished she had someone to laugh with, someone to keep. But better to be alone than to fall for a man who would break her heart.

Daisy never wanted to be strung along again. She'd wasted too much of her childhood tantalized by her father's empty promises.

More than once he'd promised her the best birthday party ever. Or a back-to-school shopping spree. Or any toy she wanted for Christmas. Each time, he drank in her eager anticipation over the phone. Yet he hardly ever showed up.

It had taken Daisy years of ruined holidays to get wise. After that, she'd refused to believe his lies, but somehow she'd managed to pick two boyfriends who turned out to be a lot like her father, all promises and no follow-through. It was happening again with Chance.

She wanted a husband and a family so badly. Why did she have to fall for someone as unattainable as Chance Foster?

No, she hadn't fallen, Daisy told herself sternly. Her skin was on fire from hormones, not passion.

Her stomach churned because she was worried about getting Shakira's exhibit ready in time for the opening. Or maybe her stomach problems, too, were the result of her hormone swings.

Daisy hoped she wasn't getting her period, not when she had such a busy day tomorrow. The endometriosis made periods painful, and she'd been glad when she skipped last month.

With a jolt, she realized that her symptoms fit a pattern. A missed period. A queasy stomach. A higher-than-normal temperature.

It couldn't be. True, two months ago, she and Chance had been so carried away that neither of them had used contraception.

But the hormones she took functioned as birth control pills. No way could she get pregnant by accident. Except...

She'd missed a couple of weeks while waiting for the mail-order prescription to be filled.

Was it possible? Much as she wanted a baby, it was unthinkable that she could be pregnant. Not now. *Not with Chance's child.*

Ahead, Daisy spotted a drugstore. If she didn't quash this crazy notion tonight, she'd never be able to sleep. Determined to put the matter to rest, she parked in front of the drugstore and went in.

PINK. It didn't look good on auburn-haired women, Daisy thought wildly, standing in her bathroom staring at the small stick in the tube. Definitely not her color. It had to be a mistake.

Maybe she'd misunderstood and pink didn't mean positive after all. Hoping against hope, she picked up the box and read it again.

"A pink color indicates the presence of hormones associated with pregnancy. Confirmation by a medical professional is recommended. This product has been shown to be 98 percent accurate."

There was, she noted with a tiny wiggle of hope, a two percent chance this test was wrong. Could her medication have created a false positive?

Then Daisy remembered something else. In case of

pregnancy, she needed to stop taking her hormones at once.

Frantically she dialed her doctor's exchange. The operator, after asking a few questions, patched her through to Dr. Adhuri.

He listened to her stumbling explanation. "I'll be in my office for a few hours tomorrow morning." The doctor occasionally came in on Saturdays to help infertility patients whose ovulation set its own schedule. "Come by at nine o'clock."

"Thanks." Trembling, she set down the phone.

Sinking onto the couch, Daisy hugged herself. She was tempted to call her mother, but then both of them would lose a night's sleep.

What was she going to do if she was pregnant? She'd always vowed not to bring up a child without a father. Should she consider adoption?

One of the artists she represented had adopted two beautiful daughters from China. Providing a baby to two loving people could turn a misfortune into a blessing, Daisy had always believed.

But she didn't know if she could give up the only child she might ever have. And it was Chance's. Whatever his failings as a potential mate, he was an intelligent, appealing man. His child would be a treasure.

Suddenly she didn't know whether she hoped she wasn't pregnant or hoped she was.

"CONGRATULATIONS," Dr. Adhuri said.

Daisy regarded him in confusion. She'd dressed after her examination but had expected the results of the urine test to take longer than a few minutes. "You mean…?"

"You're pregnant," he said. "There were positive

indications in the examination, and the test confirms
it.''

A shiver ran through her. Partly relief, partly fear.
''Will the endometriosis cause any problems?''

''It shouldn't, but we'll monitor you closely.'' The
doctor scribbled out a prescription. ''You won't need
your hormones, because your body will manufacture
plenty, but you should start taking vitamins right away.
I also recommend fish oil capsules and a healthy diet,
including plenty of eggs.''

He provided more medical advice, and then the nurse
came with informational pamphlets and made the next
appointment. No one asked about a husband, but then,
they knew she wasn't married.

When Daisy left the office, her thoughts were frag-
mented. She ought to call someone. Her mother.
Chance. But she couldn't. Not yet.

She drove to the gallery and managed to get through
putting the final touches on Shakira's exhibit. Sean had
done a professional job of hanging the show after Daisy
left on Friday, but the spotlights needed to be adjusted
and a table set up for refreshments.

By one o'clock, everything was ready. ''I have to
go out now,'' she said, finger-combing a wedge of auburn hair. ''Do I look a mess? I ought to put on lipstick. No, wait, I'm going to be trying on bridesmaids'
dresses. They could get smeared.''

''What did that fellow do to you?'' her assistant
asked with unexpected boldness. He usually didn't
meddle in Daisy's private business. Of course, she
didn't usually have any private business.

''Do to me?'' She wondered if Sean could have
guessed her secret.

"You've hardly said a word all morning and now you're chattering. Are you okay?"

"I'm fine," she said.

The young man's eyes narrowed. Clearly, he didn't believe her. "Is he coming to the opening tonight?"

"He said he was. To return the portfolio."

"I've never seen anybody make you this nervous," Sean muttered.

"I hope he wasn't wasting my time." Daisy searched for a plausible justification for her state of mind. "He seemed interested in buying, but he might turn out to be the kind of person who talks a big story."

In the year since Sean came to work here full-time, they'd dealt with two wealthy individuals who dangled their money as a lure but after a while disappeared. Like Daisy's father, such customers loved being the center of attention at other people's expense.

"I know how you hate that." Her assistant accepted the explanation. "Don't let him rattle you. You're the one who told me that kind of thing goes with the territory."

"I know." Daisy sighed. "I never get used to it, though."

She checked her watch. She'd promised to meet Phoebe and Elise at Here Comes the Bride, an elegant shop that featured the latest styles. It was time to leave.

Sean promised to lock up at five and return at seven. The guests should start arriving at eight.

"I'll see you then." With the half guilty, half pleased sense of skipping school, Daisy went through the back of the shop.

As she passed her studio, she peered inside. The half dozen Personality Pots had dried evenly and awaited bisque-firing. Normally she didn't come in on Sundays, but perhaps tomorrow she would.

Only three of the tall pots would fit in her kiln at one time, so she'd need to make several firings. An extra day's labor would speed the process.

She was excited about her work. Despite her other concerns, Daisy's spirits lifted as she set out to meet her friends.

"I DON'T CARE if lime-green is the latest color, I'm not wearing it," Phoebe announced as she and Daisy modeled their dresses in front of a mirror.

This was the third bridal shop they'd tried. So far, no luck.

"It looks great on you!" Elise protested.

And it did, Daisy mused. Lime-green brought out the highlights of Phoebe's blond hair and made her blue eyes even more vivid.

The problem was Daisy's complexion. In this hue, she resembled a tri-colored lollipop.

"I've got it!" Phoebe said. "We'll wear white."

"Excuse me?" Elise slanted her a what-are-you-up-to-now look.

Their friend assumed a newscaster's poker expression. "'The bride wore the traditional lime-green, beautifully set off by her attendants in white.' What do you think?"

"I believe 'yuck' about covers it," said the bride-to-be. "Besides, I've already got my dress."

The shop's owner emerged from the back room with two dresses wrapped in plastic. "Excuse me. These just arrived and I haven't had time to put them out yet. I thought you might be interested."

All three of them nodded. And hoped. If these

dresses didn't enchant them, they didn't know what they were going to do.

The shopkeeper peeled back the plastic and hung the two gowns on a high peg for inspection. They were coordinated but not identical, with old-fashioned necklines, flower-print insets and lace trim. One was the delicate color called ashes of roses, the other a darker shade of pink.

"They're beautiful." Phoebe plucked the darker dress and held it against herself in front of the mirror. "And flattering."

"A matching bouquet would be gorgeous, with maybe a dark-green accent," Elise said.

The shopkeeper had brought the right sizes, Daisy saw. "Let's try them on."

A few minutes later the two of them were pirouetting in their finery, posing in the showroom's large mirrors. "I can't believe how flattering this is," Phoebe said. "What do you think of having as your wedding theme 'A Garden Party'?"

"I like it," said Elise.

Studying herself in the mirror, Daisy wished Chance could see her in this feminine dress. Then she remembered that at the wedding he would.

By then how big would she be? The wedding was in September, three months away. At five months, she'd be showing.

Instinctively she smoothed her hands along the high-waisted dress. It should have ample room if she didn't gain too much weight.

"I think it will still fit," she said aloud.

Her friends stopped debating what flowers to choose and stared at her. "What do you mean?" Elise asked.

Daisy froze. She hadn't meant to say anything until she'd decided what she was going to do.

"I mean..." She stopped.

Her friends waited, fidgeting. The shopkeeper had gone to answer the phone.

There was no point in lying. Eventually she'd have to tell them the truth, anyway. "I'm pregnant," Daisy blurted out, and ran for the dressing room.

Her friends didn't pursue her. Maybe they were being discreet, but more likely they were stunned...and trying to figure out the identity of the father.

Her cheeks burning with embarrassment, Daisy removed the dress and hung it up. She couldn't answer their questions. Not yet.

What if Chance insisted on a paternity test? She knew he was the father, since she hadn't been with anyone else for over a year, but he might refuse to believe her.

Daisy straightened her shoulders. She didn't need his help. True, a man had financial obligations to his child, but she would prefer to manage by herself rather than deal with someone who didn't really want her or the baby.

And she hadn't ruled out the possibility of adoption. If she went that route, she didn't want to stir Elise's concerns about her own niece or nephew being taken away. Better if she played her cards close to her chest for now.

When she emerged, her friends were waiting. Phoebe had changed into street clothes in record time, she saw.

Two pairs of eyes brimmed with curiosity. Two pairs of lips trembled with inquiries.

"Don't even ask," Daisy said. "Are we getting these dresses? I vote yes."

The two heads nodded.

"You can't mean you aren't going to tell us who the father is," Phoebe said. "We're your best friends."

"Which means that you of all people respect my privacy," Daisy replied.

"Of course we do!" said Elise. "We wouldn't dream of telling anyone else."

"That's right." Daisy marched toward the sales desk. "You *won't* tell anyone else. Will you?"

"You mean we can't tell anyone you're…?" Phoebe stopped, noting the proximity of a mother and daughter looking at bridal gowns. "Okay. Mum's the word."

"You mean Mom's the word." Elise started to giggle, but stopped at Daisy's unamused expression. "Just a little joke."

"You can't keep it secret forever." Phoebe carried her own dress to the desk.

"I'll let you know when I decide to go public," Daisy said. She wanted her mother's advice first, and then she would break the news to Chance.

It was nearly five o'clock. Time to eat dinner and get ready for the opening. She could see her mother tomorrow.

Phoebe and Elise had promised to keep her secret. By the time she faced Chance, matters should be much clearer.

But what if Chance showed up at tonight's opening? How would she feel about him now that he was to be the father of her child?

Chapter Six

Chance spent most of Saturday preparing for his Monday court case. It took longer than usual because his thoughts kept straying to Daisy.

Surely if she'd suffered some deep-down trauma, he'd have heard about it from Elise. His sister talked freely about her friends, and Chance heard the details of their lives whether he wanted to or not.

The only thing he could recall Elise mentioning was trying in vain to matchmake for Daisy. There'd been, he recalled hearing, a date with a dentist that hadn't worked out.

She was picky, his sister said. Or were there deeper problems?

Daisy was probably a bad bet for a relationship. Too flighty, too troubled. She wasn't at all like the imaginary woman Chance had been seeking since his breakup with Gillian.

A woman serene in her self-knowledge. Open, communicative, easygoing. A woman who never surprised or worried him.

Well, he didn't have to marry Daisy. He just wanted to talk to her, inhale her scent and make her laugh. What was wrong with that?

He was finishing a frozen dinner when he decided to drop by his sister's condo on his way to the gallery. Of course, Elise might not be home, but maybe Daisy hadn't left her condo yet, and he could stop by to say hello.

After eating, Chance changed into a business suit, grabbed the portfolio and headed for town. At the Mesa Blue condos, he waved to the security guard in the lobby and, in his hurry to go upstairs, nearly tripped over a bounding calico cat.

"Watch out!" A bright kimono flowing around her, Frannie Fitzgerald rushed from unit 1B and grabbed the cat. "You nearly stepped on her!"

"She ran right in front of me," Chance protested.

"I'm sure Muffikins would never be that foolish. Are you sure you weren't being careless?" the woman demanded.

He got the feeling that she was only half-serious. From the way she kept glancing at Bill White, who had stopped to chat with the security guard, Chance figured the show was being staged for his benefit.

"I would never deliberately mow down a cat," he said, "not even such an ugly one as this." He winked at Frannie.

"Did you hear that?" she demanded of Bill.

The superintendent gazed around with a Who-me? Expression. "What?"

"He called Muffikins ugly! And he tried to run right over her. It's an obvious case of attempted cat-i-cide right in your lobby. What are you going to do about it?"

Standing on a ladder in one corner replacing a light bulb, Jeff Hawkin absorbed this interchange with a grin. Obviously, he knew what was going on.

"I suggest you keep in mind as you frame your answer that I'm a lawyer," Chance joked to the superintendent.

Bill nodded resignedly. "I have to follow the house rules, anyway. May I remind you, Frannie, you've been requested to keep your cats out of the common areas."

"This is a cat, singular, not cats, plural!" Frannie looked genuinely hurt, taking his rebuke as a personal rejection. "But don't worry. I won't bother anyone again!" Keeping a tight grip on the calico, she marched into her apartment and slammed the door.

Bill sighed. "Things are never dull when she's around. One way or another."

Lost in thought, Chance mounted the stairs. Over the years he'd come to think of the ideal marriage as a placid, comfortable state, like a Florida vacation. It hadn't occurred to him that a woman might be prized *because* she stirred things up.

Daisy certainly stirred him up. In the months since they'd met, she'd disrupted his thoughts and turned his world upside down. He wouldn't have sought out such a woman, yet now that he'd met her, he couldn't understand why he'd wasted time dating boring socialites.

From outside his sister's unit, Chance caught the scent of spaghetti sauce. Too bad he'd already eaten, he thought, and knocked loudly.

From inside came an enthusiastic "Hi!" and Elise threw open the door. Her light-brown hair was curled within an inch of its life, and she wore an emerald silk blouse over white slacks, not exactly the ideal outfit for cooking spaghetti. "Oh, it's you."

"Expecting James?"

"Well, I didn't put this on for Phoebe, much as I enjoy her company." When the door opened wider, he saw the blonde sitting on his sister's sofa, wearing a frothy pink cocktail dress.

"I'm going out with Wyatt in a few minutes," she explained. "Your sister and I had a lot to talk about." She bit her lip, as if she'd said more than she'd intended.

"Oh? What about?" Chance waited, mildly curious.

"Nothing in particular," said Phoebe.

Elise tied on an apron she'd evidently discarded just before opening the door. "We found the bridesmaids' gowns today. Isn't that wonderful?"

"Great." Whatever they'd been gossiping about, he doubted it was bridesmaids' gowns. Not that Chance cared. He'd come here to learn about Daisy's past traumas, if he could find a tactful way to broach the subject. "Was Daisy with you?"

"Of course," Phoebe said. "We could hardly buy the dresses without her."

"Oh!" Elise's eyes widened. "I'd completely forgotten. You like her, don't you?"

"Daisy?" He found himself reluctant to tell his sister too much. "She...seems nice."

"I'm afraid she's taken," Elise said.

Chance's mind clicked frantically, like a slipping cog. Taken? Since yesterday? "What do you mean?"

Phoebe shot her friend a quelling stare. "We promised not to tell!"

If Daisy had a secret boyfriend, that would explain her abrupt withdrawal from Chance's embrace. It wouldn't explain, however, how she'd come to enter that embrace in the first place. "Tell what?"

"He's my brother, for Pete's sake!" Elise said to Phoebe. "And who's he going to gossip to? He doesn't know any of her other friends."

"She said not to tell anyone," the blonde repeated doggedly.

"She meant anybody who counts."

"I'm so flattered, words fail me," Chance said dryly.

"I refuse to participate in this discussion. No offense, Chance." Getting to her feet, Phoebe brushed by him and went out the door. There was a moment of silence, and then...

"She's pregnant," Elise said.

Chance smiled. "I'm pleased for Wyatt. Of course, they should have been more careful till they're married."

"Not Phoebe! Daisy!"

The light in the room wavered. The air hurt his lungs. Chance struggled to absorb what she'd said, but he could hardly sort out his thoughts.

Two months ago he and Daisy hadn't used any protection. He'd been angry at himself later. It was the first time he'd been that careless.

After she'd vanished, however, he hadn't given the matter any further thought. One night was hardly likely to result in a pregnancy. Or so he'd assumed.

Why hadn't she told him yesterday? It was cruel to leave him to learn such earth-shattering news from a third party. Or had Daisy not meant for him to find out at all?

Chance was struggling to get his reaction under control when, following a knock, James came through the half-open door. The dark-haired man greeted his fiancée with a hug.

When they parted, Elise was beaming. She didn't seem to notice anything amiss in her brother's behavior.

"Good to see you, Chance." He and James shook hands. Despite his wealth, there was nothing pretentious about the man.

"I just stopped by," Chance heard himself say. "On my way to a social event."

"Before you go..." James glanced at Elise as if for confirmation of something, then said, "I like your idea about premarital counseling. I wouldn't embark on a new business venture without hiring a consultant, and what's more important than my marriage?"

"If you happen to have the name of a counselor, we'd appreciate it." Elise brushed a bit of lint from James's sleeve. Taking care of him already, Chance noted.

From his wallet he retrieved the card of a psychologist to whom he frequently referred clients. "I can recommend this counselor."

"Thanks." James pocketed the card.

After a few more pleasantries, Chance made it into the hall. A couple of deep breaths steeled his nerves before he rang Daisy's bell at the adjacent unit.

No answer.

Had she heard his voice next door? Was she pulling another disappearing act?

He checked his watch. It was after seven. She must have left for the gallery.

Chance didn't want to confront her in public. On the other hand, he needed to return the portfolio and was eager to meet the artist. And to see how Daisy looked.

He wasn't sure what, if anything, he would say to her tonight. But he couldn't stay away.

A KNOT OF FASCINATED people gathered around Shakira Benjamin. Although the African-American woman was of average height and wore simple dresses, her lively face and energetic manner made her the center of attention.

Daisy smiled, pleased that the reception was going so well. More than fifty guests circulated through the gallery, studying the new exhibit and enjoying the wine, punch, cheese and crackers.

Helen and Rolland Madison stopped by to say hello. The eighty-something couple lived in Mesa Blue down the hall from Phoebe and were responsible for introducing her to her future husband, their grandson Wyatt.

"I love visiting your gallery!" Helen, a retired teacher who wore her salt-and-pepper hair very short, appeared much younger than her years. "It reminds me of the museums Rolland and I visited in France."

The couple had traveled a good deal during Rolland's career in the Navy. Daisy always enjoyed hearing their reminiscences.

"It doesn't bear much resemblance to the Louvre," teased her husband, whose military bearing made him appear even taller than he was. "Or—what's that palace?—Versailles."

"I didn't mean that!" His wife rapped his hand with a brochure. "I meant the smaller galleries in the south of France. The Matisse Museum, for instance."

Daisy hadn't been able to travel abroad, much as she would love to see the places she'd read about. "The farthest I've gone is New York, and a few trips to Los Angeles," she admitted.

Behind the couple a tall man entered the gallery. A subtle tension ran through her. Chance. He'd come, but he didn't look happy about it.

With a nod of acknowledgment, he set the portfolio on the front table and headed for the exhibit. Absorbed, he stood for several minutes in front of each painting before moving on to the next.

Could he have been serious about making purchases? For Shakira's sake, Daisy hoped so.

"When you meet the right man, you can travel with him," Helen said. "There's nothing more romantic than seeing the marvels of the world with a person you love."

"As long as the plumbing works," Rolland added with a wink. "That isn't always the case over there, you know."

Sean arrived from the storage room with refills for the nut bowls, and new guests claimed Daisy's attention. It was half an hour before Chance approached.

She couldn't read anything in his expression. The man must be a great poker player.

"I'd like to buy the painting of the two Native American children," he said. "It isn't already sold, is it?"

Daisy shook her head. Shakira's canvases ran from $8,000 to $10,000 each, and this was the most expensive. She'd only made one other sale this evening, of a smaller work. "I'd be happy to write it up for you."

"Great." From his inside coat pocket, Chance withdrew a checkbook. He didn't waste time, she thought.

"It will have to remain on display for the duration of the exhibit," Daisy said as she logged the payment. "Of course we'll label it sold and deliver it to your home as soon as the show comes down. Or to your office, if you prefer."

"Home," he said.

It wasn't like Chance to speak so tersely. Daisy searched his expression again. She didn't think he was angry, but some emotion was definitely at work.

"I guess you're annoyed about yesterday, huh?" she asked when no one was nearby.

"No."

"What, then?"

"We'll talk about this later," he said.

"Talk about what?"

"Your condition," he said, and walked away.

Daisy's hands went cold. There was no mistaking his point. Elise must have spilled the truth.

This was the worst possible way for Chance to learn about it. He had a right to be upset.

Daisy stumbled through the rest of the evening. A collector bought another of Shakira's paintings, and the art critic for an alternative newspaper collected information about the painter's background. From his questions Daisy gathered he was impressed.

Operating on automatic pilot, she wished the guests well as they departed, congratulated Shakira and worked with Sean to clear away the refreshments. "I'll stop by tomorrow and finish straightening," she told him when they were done. "Go home. Or go play. Whatever you do on Saturday nights."

"Play, of course." With a grin, off he went.

Only Chance remained, lingering in Gallery II, an exhibit of sculpture by three artists inspired by the Arizona desert landscape. At his house, Daisy had mentioned the cactus-like metal creations as possibilities to add height to the front planter area. She didn't suppose he was planning to make another purchase tonight, though.

When she couldn't delay any longer, she ventured into the gallery. He was facing away from her. "You've been talking to Elise?"

His back stiffened, and he nodded.

"I was going to tell you tomorrow," Daisy said. "I just found out today."

At that, Chance turned. "It wasn't the reason you left yesterday?"

"No," she said. "I was feeling overheated and queasy. On my way home I realized what the symptoms meant. The doctor confirmed it this morning."

Poised among the jagged metallic sculptures, Chance stared at her like a wild creature trapped in headlights. He had an edginess unlike his usual self.

"Is it mine?" he asked.

"Of course!" she said. "You see...the problem started..." She sucked in a deep breath. "I take hormones for endometriosis."

"I know," he said. "Elise told me."

The woman was a dear friend, but she had a loose mouth, Daisy thought ruefully. "The hormones act like birth control pills," she went on. "I wasn't thinking. When I changed prescriptions, I was off the hormone pills briefly and temporarily lost my protection. I'm sorry."

"It's as much my fault as..." He stopped. "This isn't a question of affixing blame."

"No, it isn't." Daisy began to pace. Her feet pinched from the medium-heeled shoes she'd worn with her mid-calf, print dress, but she couldn't stand still. "I haven't decided what to do. I wanted to sleep on it before I called you."

"You haven't decided what to do?" Chance repeated. "This is as much my decision as yours."

She couldn't believe his nerve. "No, it isn't. I realize you're affected, but I have to take most of the consequences myself. If I keep the child, I'll be raising it alone just as my mother did. If I give it up..."

"You're talking about adoption?" he said. "I have no problem with adoption. In fact, I find it very rewarding to help people through the legal process. But you don't have to do this. You're not a young girl, and you have resources. Including me."

Oh? And how long will you stick around after you find high-gloss, high-achieving Ms. Perfect? she wondered.

Aloud she said, "My father started out promising to take care of me, too. His resolve didn't last long."

"I'm not your father."

Daisy had to admit Chance was entitled to be judged by his own actions. "If I decide to keep the baby, of course you can be involved."

He shook his head. "That isn't enough."

"What do you mean?"

"We'll get married. It's the right thing to do."

She could see the strain on his face. It hurt to realize how much the prospect pained him. "Isn't that an old-fashioned idea?"

"It's an honorable idea." Chance regarded her steadily. "We owe it to our child."

If only he wanted to be her husband for a different reason! If he loved her...but he didn't. And she couldn't marry him just for the child's sake.

Her body already craved him. If they married, she would fall in love, and he would break her heart. Tromp on it, crush it and shatter it into a million pieces.

"I'm not a charity case," she said.

"Don't be stubborn!" Chance folded his arms commandingly. "It's my job to take care of you and our baby."

"No," Daisy said.

"I could take you to court over this."

The threat knocked the air from her lungs. She couldn't afford an attorney as skillful as Chance. If he sued for custody, he would win.

"If you do, I'll move out of state," she said. "I won't let you run my life, or my child's."

"Moving won't shield you from a custody battle."

They squared off, each anxiously waiting for the other to make the first move. Chance blinked a couple of times, as if awakening from a daze, and the tautness eased from his stance. "I didn't mean that, Daisy. I'm sorry. My sisters tell me I'm overly controlling, and they're right."

She released a long breath and admitted a truth she hadn't wanted to acknowledge until now. "I suppose you'd have to sign adoption papers before they were finalized, anyway."

"That's right."

"So we need to reach an agreement." She still couldn't believe that she and a man had came to the brink of a bitter argument yet managed to avoid it. This was a new experience.

Chance ran his hand over a mock organ-pipe cactus made of wire. "It's true that we don't know each other very well. And I have high standards for marriage. But I think two mature, sensible people who go into it with their eyes open can make it work."

How typical of a lawyer to make his case with logic instead of emotion. "What about love?" Daisy said. "Isn't that essential to a marriage?"

"I used to think so." He stared into the distance. "A divorce lawyer sees the worst of the worst. It amazes me how quickly love fades in the face of financial difficulties, boredom, frustration and resentment."

"Your solution is to marry a woman you don't love?" Daisy couldn't believe the twisted rationale.

He gave her a startled look. "I didn't mean it that way."

"You're as confused as I am," she said.

Slowly he smiled. "I guess I am. But don't think I'm backing down."

"Chance, I appreciate your concern, but I need to work through this situation in my own way," Daisy said. "I've never leaned on anyone, and I don't intend to start now."

She switched off the spotlights in the gallery, leaving only the baseboard-level safety lights. He followed as she walked through the rooms, shutting everything down.

"I think we should get married, but I can't force you," he said. "In any case I'm going to be part of my child's life every step of the way. Starting now."

"I fail to see how you can interact with a baby that hasn't been born yet."

"I can accompany you to the doctor." Chance stayed close, without crowding her. "Get your prescriptions filled. Make sure you're eating properly. Take childbirth classes with you."

"And deliver the baby yourself?" she teased.

"If they'll let me." He wasn't kidding.

Daisy wondered how long this solicitude would last. She'd never been through a pregnancy, and neither had any of her close friends, but she'd read enough to know that women were often irritable and achy.

"I might let you give me back rubs," she conceded.

"No problem. I'll take care of your expenses, too. Including doctor bills." Chance warmed to his subject.

"You'll need a maternity wardrobe, right? And baby supplies."

"As far as the doctor's concerned, I accept." The cost would be at least several thousand dollars, Daisy knew. "I can handle my other expenses."

"We'll see about that."

She locked the front door from the inside, crossed the nearly dark gallery and exited through the rear. He followed.

Chance, she saw when they got outside, had parked next to her station wagon. "I'm going to see my mother tomorrow. I want her advice about adoption."

"What time do you think you'll talk to her?"

"She'll probably invite me for brunch," Daisy said.

"I'll drop by your place in the afternoon. Around three?"

"I'll be here working." He wasn't shy about inviting himself over, she thought. "I'll call you when I've made my decision."

He drummed his fingers on the roof of his sports car. "Daisy…"

Not another argument! "What?"

"What was wrong with him?" he asked. "The dentist."

"What dentist?"

"The one my sister fixed you up with," he said. "I've been wondering."

Good heavens, she'd almost forgotten the man. "He was too materialistic," Daisy said. "All he cared about were things."

"I'm not like that." After she unlocked her car, Chance held the door for her. "I care about the baby. And you."

She supposed he meant it, in his own way. "We'll talk," she said. "When I'm ready."

Reluctantly Chance closed the door. She drove off with a lingering image of his intense watchfulness in the rear-view mirror.

Chapter Seven

On Sunday morning Jeanine Redford's kitchen smelled of honey-bran muffins, turkey bacon and coffee. Daisy wolfed down the food but, to her disappointment, she no longer found the smell of coffee appetizing.

She'd been looking forward to her mother's fresh-ground French roast. Instead she drank tea.

"It's your hormones," her mother explained. "They're guiding you to healthier eating."

"Then how come I crave sugar?"

"Well, hormones aren't perfect," said her mother.

Daisy had blurted out her news the moment she entered the fabric-and-notion-cluttered adobe house in Tempe. Jeanine took the revelation without scolding. She was delighted at the prospect of a grandchild, if not at the absence of a husband.

They ate on plates Daisy had made herself years ago. To her more mature eye, they looked too thick and the glaze was overbright, but her mother prized her set of homemade dishes above anything store bought.

Now Jeanine led the way into the living room. As she walked, her long gray-streaked brown hair swung in a loose knot, gathered near the bottom. Daisy had never seen anyone else wear her hair that way.

It must be a leftover hippie style. Her mother had been a free spirit in her younger days. Still was, come to think of it.

When Daisy was a teenager, she'd worried about how little money they had, with only dribs and drabs coming in from Jeanine's seamstress work. They needed to be free, her mother had answered.

You never knew when opportunity might knock. Life was full of potential. She might meet someone exciting, and perhaps they would get a chance to travel. But they never did.

A small inheritance from Daisy's grandparents had tided them over. Eventually Jeanine's income rose as she began designing costumes for dancers and theater companies.

Despite the haphazard appearance of the living room, Daisy knew her mother had everything under control. Otherwise she could never have designed and cut and stitched dozens of costumes and finished them on time for performances.

"So Elise's brother offered to marry you." Jeanine transferred a pile of cut fabric pieces from the sofa to the coffee table. "He sounds like a gentleman."

"He is." Daisy dusted away a few loose threads before sitting down. Her jeans felt tight, perhaps from the meal. Surely the baby couldn't be growing that fast! "But I don't want to be a wife in name only. I want a real husband."

Her mother smiled dreamily. "Times have changed. Back in the Seventies, we considered marriage an out-dated institution. We thought we could reinvent the world."

"Did my father ask you to marry him?"

"If Mick had proposed, I'd have keeled over in a

faint!'' Jeanine rescued a glittery button from between two couch cushions. ''He was a musician, you know. Always heading out with a gig, only now he plays country instead of acid rock.''

''Do you keep in touch with him?'' she asked. Daisy hadn't talked to her father in years.

Jeanine shrugged. ''He calls once in a while. For old-time's sake, and to ask about you. I guess it's a way of hanging on to the connections we made when we were young.''

Daisy had heard the story of her mother's youth many times, in bits and pieces. How Jeanine left Phoenix at eighteen for Los Angeles, seeking costuming work at movie studios. How she and a group of aspiring artists, writers and musicians had shared a house in the Silverlake district.

Looking back, Daisy could see that it was her mother's daring attitude that had given Daisy the courage to launch a gallery when most people thought she was too young. She'd started seven years ago in an out-of-the-way storefront on a month-to-month lease, two years later moved to a Scottsdale location, and to her present spot three years ago.

She supposed she could instead have sought the most secure job possible, with regular paychecks and benefits. That way of life had never even occurred to Daisy, and she was glad now that it hadn't.

''Chance is different from Dad,'' she said. ''I mean, obviously, he's a lawyer and earns good money, but he's a different kind of person, too.''

''He sounds a lot more stable.'' Her mother folded her hands atop her long denim skirt. ''Is he boring?''

''Chance? Never!'' The words that came to mind

were *"riveting"* and *"powerful,"* although she didn't care to describe him that way to her mother.

Daisy almost wished she hadn't turned down his suggestion that they meet later today. Except it had been more a command than a suggestion.

"Good. I'd hate for my grandchild to inherit boring genes." Her mother began sorting the cut pieces on the coffee table. "It sounds as if you like this man."

"Mom! I wouldn't have slept with him if I didn't."

Jeanine chuckled. "I meant it sounds as if you've grown attached. Could that be why you don't want to be his wife in name only?"

Glumly Daisy nodded. "I'm afraid that sooner or later he'd fall for someone else and want a divorce. It's better not to get started."

"Or he might fall in love with you," her mother said.

"I wouldn't count on it."

Jeanine's fingers drummed on the coffee table, and then she dived beneath it and came up with a piece of fabric that had fallen to the carpet. "You said you wanted advice. Not about marrying him, I gather?"

"No, about the baby." Daisy consulted her mother whenever she had a major decision to make. She didn't always follow the suggestions, but they helped clarify her thinking. "Mom, I know that having a child alone, much as you love me, wasn't easy. You had to sacrifice a lot."

During the pregnancy, Jeanine had moved back to Phoenix to live with her widowed mother and had stayed to nurse her through a final illness. She'd never returned to L.A., never landed that dream job assisting a major studio designer.

"I wouldn't change a thing," her mother said. "Besides, for you things are different. You're thirty. I was twenty-one. You've established a reputation and a business. I had barely started."

"You don't think I should consider adoption?" Daisy asked.

"Only if you want to very strongly." Sunlight flooding between the slats of the miniblinds brought out the steely strands in Jeanine's once-chestnut hair. "The years go by quickly, you know. This may be your only child."

She refrained from adding "and my only grandchild," but Daisy knew she was thinking it. Besides, now that she'd told her friends and her mother and Chance, the baby seemed to belong to all of them, not just to her.

A fierce swell of love surged through her for the tiny being inside. The feeling scared her with its ferocity.

Where had this come from? Was it being in her mother's house, filled with memories of childhood, that had awakened it?

"I guess I've made up my mind," Daisy said. "I want to keep my child, although I'm not sure I'm prepared for what that's going to mean."

One thing it meant, she acknowledged silently, was that Chance Foster would always have a claim on the most precious person in her world. He was going to be part of her life whether she liked it or not.

She would have to watch as the years went by and he fell in love with a woman like his former fiancée, a top-notch, hard-driving professional. Perhaps it would be the blond woman Daisy had seen outside the restaurant.

They would drive up to Mesa Blue and collect the

little girl, or boy, for the weekend. Smiling and linking arms. Barely noticing Daisy.

Her chest squeezed. She would get used to it, she told herself. Perhaps even find a mate for herself—a gentle, mild-mannered fellow who could accept another man's child.

Her mother never had. But Daisy was different.

"Pregnancy does that," her mother said.

"Does what?"

"Makes your mind wander. It makes you sleep a lot, too, and very deeply."

As if on cue, Daisy yawned. The she laughed. "I'm not tired! It's the power of suggestion."

"You're not going to push this man away from the child, are you?" Jeanine said, returning to their earlier topic of conversation. "I'm not sorry that Mick occasionally dropped by and called, even though he disappointed both of us and spoiled a lot of holidays. It would have been worse if you'd never known him."

That was true. Daisy had needed to come to terms with her imperfect father.

She'd last seen him five years earlier. In town to perform at a club in Phoenix, he'd dropped by her booth at the Scottsdale Celebration of Fine Arts.

She'd invited him to the opening of her second gallery, which represented a giant advance from her first storefront establishment. He'd promised to attend, since the date was only a few days away.

He hadn't come. He hadn't even cared enough to call and apologize.

The hurt had abated after a while. As an adult Daisy understood that her father's selfishness implied no deficiencies on her part.

Mick had never grown up and never would. After

that last experience, she'd said goodbye to childhood fantasies about someday having a strong relationship with her father.

There was an empty space, though, where her dad should have been. Daisy was certain Chance, already a devoted older brother, wouldn't behave that way toward his own child. Even if she couldn't have him for herself, he would make a good parent.

"Well?" said Jeanine.

"I won't push him away." It was the most she could promise.

CHANCE SPENT SUNDAY orningm at his family's church. He especially enjoyed, after the service, seeing his young nieces and nephews and catching up on his parents' and sisters' lives.

He pictured himself bringing his own child here, in Daisy's arms. Greeting the friendly relatives, sharing his pleasure in this miracle.

And it was a miracle. The more he thought about it, the more he wondered why he hadn't been eager to have a child long ago. Maybe it was because he hadn't met Daisy.

He admired her strength and her forthrightness. It had never even occurred to her to use their baby as a bargaining chip to try to squeeze money out of him. His impulsive offer of marriage, at which many women would have jumped for self-serving reasons, hadn't tempted her at all.

So now he was flattered because a woman refused his proposal? Chance had to smile.

After eating lunch with his family, he went home, changed clothes and tried to relax with a travel book, Paul Theroux's *The Pillars of Hercules*. The author's eccentric trip around the Mediterranean held his interest only fitfully today, though, because his thoughts kept drifting to Daisy.

Had she made a decision? If so, did she plan to tell her friends before she told him?

It was after two o'clock. She'd mentioned working today, which presumably meant handling administrative details at the gallery. Chance decided to drop by.

Surely she wouldn't mind interrupting her paperwork for a brief chat. In any case, he wanted to know what she'd decided.

DAISY LOWERED the heavy lid of the kiln and switched it on. It would take six to eight hours to reach 1800 degrees, then cool for another fourteen to eighteen hours before she could see the results.

The three character pots that hadn't fitted into this firing sat on the table, awaiting their turn tomorrow. One resembled Frannie Fitzgerald; a second was identifiable as a sarcastic TV personality; the third was modeled after one of Daisy's least favorite politicians.

Now she had all afternoon to create new ones. Humming to herself, Daisy removed a large chunk of clay from a plastic bag and began wedging it on another table. She kneaded the clay hard to remove air bubbles.

It was a relief to have made up her mind about the baby, she reflected as she worked. She still couldn't fully grasp everything that was happening to her body and her life, but for today she felt at peace.

As she worked, her mind filled with images. A cooing baby held to her breast. A toddler plopping into a sandbox and digging with a plastic shovel. A little girl or boy holding up chubby arms and saying, "I wuv you, Mommy."

Mommy. That precious title was going to be hers.

The people at Mesa Blue might be dubious at first about her unwed state, but she knew they'd adore the baby. The Madisons, who had raised their grandson after the unexpected death of their son, would insist on baby-sitting.

As for Phoebe and Elise, they'd probably have babies of their own soon. The children could play together, grow up together.

But your friends will have husbands and you won't.

Daisy stopped wedging the clay, which, she realized, she'd begun pounding in a fury. She ought to take out her frustrations on the potter's wheel before her arms got too tired.

Last Monday she'd enjoyed bashing Chance in effigy. Why not do it again? He would never know the difference, and it might relieve her tension.

A little guiltily, she set to work making a small bust of the man.

DAISY'S STATION WAGON sat in its accustomed spot behind the gallery. Good, Chance thought. She was here.

He parked and walked to the service entrance. Inside, the buzzer sounded.

It took a several minutes for her to respond. He was beginning to wonder whether something was wrong, when he heard her say, "Who is it?"

"It's me, Chance."

There followed a pause so long he began to doubt she was going to let him in. Then a lock clicked and the door opened.

"Hi." She peered at him through a fringe of auburn hair. The smudge of mud on one cheek reminded him of her disheveled appearance last Monday.

"I thought you were doing paperwork." He frowned. "Are you cleaning the place?"

"I was working. I'm a potter." Daisy stepped back with a trace of reluctance.

That must be why she'd taken so long to respond to the buzzer. Curious, Chance took her hand and examined it. The skin was pink, as if newly scrubbed, and traces of clay clung to the tiny crevices and beneath her short fingernails. "You're not kidding."

"Did you think I was making it up?" she demanded.

She looked so cute, half-annoyed and clearly caught off guard by his visit, that he wanted to hug her. He doubted she'd be pleased, though. "Why didn't I see any of your work in the gallery?"

Daisy made a wry face. "Because it isn't good enough," she said. "I only display the best."

Chance considered asking point-blank what she'd decided about the baby, since that was the reason he'd come. But then they might argue and she'd throw him out.

First he wanted to learn more about her. "May I see what you're doing?"

"I don't have anything ready to show," she blurted out.

"Show me what you're working on," he said. "I don't mind if it's unfinished."

"My workshop's a mess," Daisy said. "I'll tell you what. Let me clean up a little before you come in."

She was stalling him. "What are you hiding?" he asked, amused.

"Nothing worth seeing." She squirmed like a kid.

Chance ran one hand lightly across her cheek. "No one has any right to be so pretty when she's half-covered with clay."

"I'll bet you say that to all the potters."

"Only one." He grazed her lips lightly with his own. She tasted of honey. "I'll take more of that, thank you."

"No." Daisy stepped back, her skin flushed and her eyes snapping. "I've got to get back to work before the clay dries."

"Then don't let me stop you." Chance wondered why he had deliberately tried to provoke her with a surprise kiss.

When he was with Daisy, he said and did things that startled even him. Perhaps because he loved seeing her reactions.

Flustered, she retreated across the entry space and into what appeared to be a storage room. When he followed, Chance discovered a fully equipped potter's studio.

Peripherally, he took in the kiln and potter's wheel and the shelves of chemicals. What drew his attention were three vases, each bearing a recognizable caricature. "That's the cat lady!" He identified the other two faces as well.

"It's a new idea I'm trying." Daisy stood partially blocking his view of the table. "I think I'll call them Personality Pots."

"What's behind you?" he asked.

"Nothing," she said.

Gently but firmly Chance drew her aside. What sat behind her wasn't a vase but a small sculpted bust about the right size for a large doll.

It had his face.

Puzzled, he studied it. A flattering portrait, except for a hint of smugness around the mouth. "Is that what I look like?"

"Sometimes," she said.

"Why did you make it?"

"Emotional therapy," she said.

"You're not going to put me on a vase, are you?" he asked.

Daisy's shoulders sagged. "I already did."

"Excuse me?"

She pointed at the kiln. "It's firing. Don't worry. I'm not going to display it or anything. These are purely experimental."

"They're exceptional." Chance wasn't sure he liked starring on what was probably an unflattering piece of sculpture, but he had to be fair. "If the ones in the kiln are as good as these three, you ought to display them. In fact, I might buy the one of myself. How do you think it would look in my living room?"

"I'll give it to you," Daisy said. "When it's glazed, which won't be for another week."

"I wasn't asking for a freebie." As she opened her mouth to argue, he said, "By the way, what did you decide about the baby?"

Her eyes widened and her jaw dropped. It was fun catching her by surprise.

After a moment she said, "I'm keeping it."

"Have you reconsidered my proposal?"

"No." Daisy moved the little bust to a shelf, as if to put it out of sight and out of mind. "But you're the father, and he or she needs you. Or will someday."

He nearly sagged with relief at the discovery that he wouldn't have to fight her over an adoption. But the battle was far from over.

"It's okay if you don't want to get married. All the same, we can move you into my house tomorrow,"

Chance said. "I'm due in court in the morning, but I'll take the afternoon off."

"What are you talking about?" she asked.

"You need someone around at all times." One of Chance's sisters had suffered unexpected bleeding during her first pregnancy, requiring her husband to drive her to the hospital in the middle of the night. "I've got two spare bedrooms, so there's plenty of space, and we can commute together. That way you won't be alone."

"I'm not alone!" Daisy flared. "In case you've forgotten, Elise lives next door."

"She's getting married in three months," he pointed out.

"Then three months from now, we can discuss this," she said.

Chance fixed his sternest gaze on this stubborn woman. "You'd be much safer with me."

"Would I?" she demanded. "I'd have been even safer if I'd never gone to your house in the first place!"

"That's irrelevant and illogical."

"You sound like Mr. Spock from *Star Trek*!"

"I sound like a lawyer," he retorted. "Which is what I am."

"Well, counselor, the jury verdict is in, and it's unanimous in my favor!" As if her point needed emphasis, she walked to the shelf, grabbed the little bust of him and squished it.

Chance couldn't believe she was taking out her anger on a helpless piece of clay. "That wasn't necessary."

"Be grateful I didn't stick pins in it!"

She obviously wouldn't be moving in with him tomorrow. At this point Chance wasn't sure he wanted her to.

He'd never fought this way with a woman. Calm discussion was more his style and, in his view, more productive.

"I won't let you shut me out," he said. "I'm going with you to the doctor and I'm paying the bills."

Daisy took a deep breath, clearly fighting to calm herself. "I said okay before and I meant it."

"That's better. It's important for us to discuss matters like civilized people," Chance said.

"I am civilized! Even when I'm furious, I'm civilized!" she roared. "Even if I call you horrible names and throw things at you, I'm civilized. Passivity and submission are *not* my idea of civilization!"

He could swear flames flickered in Daisy's eyes. Evidently, his remark had struck a nerve.

He wanted to reassure her, but her temper appeared to be fraying rapidly. "I'll keep in touch," Chance said, and headed out.

He was relieved, but a little surprised, that he made it through the back door without any pottery smashing into his head.

Chapter Eight

Maybe she *had* gotten carried away, Daisy conceded as she pulled up her fourth vase of the day on the potter's wheel. Smashing the effigy in front of Chance had been tactless, to say the least.

Still, she'd never been involved with a man with whom she could discuss things calmly. It didn't seem natural, when her emotions were so strongly aroused.

She'd felt backed into a corner by the demand that she move in with him. It was unthinkable to give him that much control over her life.

As she cleaned the studio after finishing work, Daisy remembered that she'd promised to meet Elise and Phoebe for dinner tonight at The Prickly Pear, a bar and grill near their condo complex. She had to hurry and change out of her clay-smeared work clothes.

She didn't want to be late. As usual these days, she was starving. And it was time to tell her friends what they most wanted to know.

ALTHOUGH THE THREE WOMEN saw each other frequently, they always had plenty to talk about. Much of it this summer concerned weddings.

Phoebe's work as a beauty consultant, and her heavy

load of biochemistry classes had made her and Wyatt decide to postpone their ceremony until late fall, she told the others as they waited to be seated. Besides, she didn't want her plans to conflict with Elise's.

"This way I can benefit from your experiences, too," she said.

Elise nodded. "I'm learning new stuff every day. You wouldn't believe the choices I have to make about the catering!"

Usually the French professor taught or traveled during summer vacation. This year, except for writing a paper for publication, she was devoting her time to the wedding.

"I'll hire you as my unpaid consultant," Phoebe said. "I'm sure your advice will be invaluable."

"You can pick any colors you like for your own ceremony," Elise offered with mock generosity. "I promise not to impose my taste."

"Is that a dig because I tried to pick yours?"

"Take it any way you like."

"Chartreuse and orange," said Phoebe. "Those are the colors I want."

"You're kidding!"

Her friend grinned. "Just wanted to see your reaction."

Neither noticed Daisy's subdued air. As they scanned their menus, she wondered how to tell them about Chance.

It was humiliating to admit she'd fallen for Mr. Charm despite Elise's cautions. But if she didn't tell them, his sister would find out from him directly, and that would be worse.

Their waiter, as usual, was George, a cheerful college student. "Hello, loves!" he declared. "Having the usual?"

That meant the chicken Caesar salad. Phoebe and Elise nodded.

"I'd like a portobello mushroom sandwich with steamed vegetables and a Caesar salad on the side," Daisy said.

"She's eating for two," Phoebe announced proudly, and then clapped her hand over her mouth at the realization that she'd blurted a secret. It was too late to take it back, though.

"Congratulations," George told Daisy. To her relief he didn't pursue the subject. "Would you ladies like anything to drink?"

Iced tea was the beverage of choice and milk for Daisy. After he departed, Elise said, "I'm surprised that James wants us to try premarital counseling. There must be something to it, though. My brother claims it saves some of his clients' marriages."

"You'd think he would want them to get divorced," Phoebe said. "He'd make more money that way."

"Chance feels it's his moral obligation," Elise said.

"Moral obligation?" Phoebe cocked an eyebrow. "An attorney?"

"You'd better not make lawyer jokes around my brother!" Elise said. "His sense of humor doesn't stretch that far."

"I promise not to tease him too hard," said Phoebe.

Their drinks arrived. Daisy seized her opportunity. "I want to tell you...about...well..."

"Yes?" Phoebe said.

"About the baby's father."

Her friends turned to stare at her. They wore twin

expressions of an almost comical earnestness, as if they scarcely dared blink.

Daisy gathered her courage. She had to force out the words quickly or she'd lose her nerve. "It's, uh, him."

"Him who?" asked Elise.

"Your—" The word *brother* stuck in her throat. Grabbing her glass, Daisy gulped the milk. It took the wrong path, and she erupted into a wrenching series of coughs.

Elise patted her on the back. Phoebe urged more milk on her.

"What were you going to say?" Elise asked.

"It's your—" she began again, and broke off to hack away.

"Neighbor?" Phoebe said helpfully. "Wait. Nobody at Mesa Blue fills the bill.

"Old friend?" Elise guessed.

"Not your assistant, that cute little Sean character!" Still gasping, Daisy shook her head.

"Someone at the university? Someone I work with?" Elise asked. Another headshake.

"By 'your,' did you mean Elise, or me?" asked Phoebe.

Daisy gulped more milk and pointed at Elise.

"I'm out of ideas," said her friend. "The only other man I can think of is my brother, and the two of you hardly—" Elise stopped. She must be remembering that day at the pool when he'd escorted Daisy away with a proprietary air. "Not Chance!"

She nodded.

Into the void stepped George with their salads. "I'll have your sandwich in just a minute," he told Daisy. "Everybody okay here?"

No one moved.

"We're famous for our coma-inducing iced tea," he said. "I can see that you're all really absorbed in the conversation, so I'm going away now. Signal if you need anything." Off he went.

"Remind me to tip him extra," said Phoebe.

Elise's mouth worked as she stared at Daisy. At last she indicated the not-yet-protruding abdomen. "You mean I've got a niece or a nephew in there?"

"Yes."

"Just for curiosity's sake, have you lost your powers of speech permanently?" Phoebe asked.

"It's temporary," Daisy choked out.

"How did this happen?" When she didn't receive an immediate answer, Elise smacked herself on the forehead. "Cancel that question. I'm well aware of how these things work. I mean when. And why?"

"I thought your medication was like birth control pills," Phoebe said.

"I went off it while I was waiting for a new prescription." It relieved Daisy to find that her voice had returned. "It was the night of your engagement party, Elise."

"So that's where you disappeared to!" said Phoebe.

"What does Chance have to say about this? Oh!" Elise cried. "I'm the one who told him, aren't I? Daisy, I'm sorry! I didn't realize—I just mentioned that you were—I didn't know he…"

There was no point in scolding. "I was going to tell him soon anyway," she said.

"How did he react?" Elise said.

"He asked me to marry him, but I said no, because he was just being polite."

"I'll bet he's crazy about you," Phoebe said loyally. "How could he help it?"

For the rest of the meal Daisy's friends plied her with support, encouragement and offers of help. This wasn't going to be so bad, she thought, her spirits rising. With their backing, she would manage.

She would rather have the support of a man she loved, who loved her in return. But she didn't intend to waste time on idle daydreams.

CHANCE STARED AT the papers on his desk without seeing them. A month had passed since he found out he was going to be a father, but nothing was settled. He wished he understood why not.

Daisy remained pleasant but aloof. When he'd dropped by the gallery, flowers in hand, she'd greeted him with professional aplomb.

She had behaved with utmost courtesy as he purchased a metal cactus sculpture, and she'd cheerfully arranged for him to tour the studios of several artists. Yet she avoided personal contact, including any but the most superficial discussion of her pregnancy.

In answer to his questions, she admitted to suffering from morning sickness. She said she was swimming these days instead of jogging. And she waved away an offer to pay for her maternity clothes, which her mother was making.

Chance wanted to know more. How did it feel to have life growing inside her? Did she wonder, as he did, what their child would be like?

Whenever he tried to broach such matters, she changed the subject. Then two days ago she'd called and asked him to accompany her to the doctor's office this afternoon to watch her ultrasound.

It was, she'd said, a key moment that he had a right

to share. Not exactly a heartfelt invitation, but it was a start.

Excitement had been building in Chance all morning. This afternoon he would see his child for the first time. It was hard even to imagine such a miracle.

After a tap at the door, Nell stuck her head inside. "Your eleven-o'clock is here," she said. "It's Mr. Abner Ewing."

"Show him in, please." Mr. Ewing, a new client, had said on the phone that he wished to initiate divorce proceedings.

Chance stood as the man entered. Slightly above average height, the client had a beefy build beneath his lightweight summer suit. Late thirties, hair thinning, expression impatient.

They shook hands, and Abner proceeded to tell his story in angry bursts. His wife of ten years had gone to her mother's house, taking their two young children.

"Janet says I'm never there. Well, of course not! I work long hours." He owned a computer repair shop. "Who bought her a beautiful house? Who's paying for private school? And this is the thanks I get!"

"I always recommend counseling to my clients," Chance said. "Everyone's better off if the issues can be resolved, whether or not you end up divorcing."

"What issues?" the man demanded, mopping his forehead with a tissue, although the office was air-conditioned against the July heat. "Janet went home to her mother. As far as I'm concerned, she needs to apologize and move back."

"There are usually two sides to a story," Chance said mildly.

"Not in this case!" Abner roared. "Janet doesn't deserve a hardworking husband like me. Lots of women would envy her a man who doesn't drink, doesn't cheat and brings home plenty of money. If she doesn't appreciate me, I'll find someone who will. Now tell me what I have to do to get a divorce!''

With an inward sigh, Chance outlined the legal process. When he was done, he again urged counseling.

"No way!" the man said. "I'm not at fault here. Let's proceed with the paperwork."

Chance complied, while privately vowing to take things as slowly as possible. Once the man's outrage cooled, he might see things differently. Or maybe not.

After Abner left, Chance ate lunch at his desk and then went to collect Daisy. He looked forward to seeing her. When she was around the air sparkled and he felt more alive.

She must have been watching through the gallery door, because she emerged the moment he pulled to the curb. A beige linen dress flowed around her like a summer cloud.

Daisy eased into his sports car wearing a polite smile. Chance ached to erase the distance between them by cupping her heart-shaped face in his hand and kissing her. This was not a good time to risk annoying her, though.

He missed the happy, outgoing woman he'd met three months ago at his sister's engagement party. He missed her so keenly it was like a knife twisting inside.

If Daisy missed their former intimacy, she showed no sign of it. She gave directions to the doctor's office as coolly as if he were a taxi driver.

The office was about a mile away through heavy traffic, which allowed them a few minutes to talk. Chance didn't intend to waste the opportunity.

"I saw a new client today," he said while navigating around a double-parked car. "His wife left him because he works all the time."

He glanced at Daisy, who appeared reflective in the muted July sunlight coming through the tinted windshield. "Do they love each other?"

"I don't know," he admitted. "What I kept thinking was, I don't want to be an absentee father like he is. I want to watch my children grow up."

"My dad told my mom the same thing," she said.

Anger spurted inside Chance. Did she have to keep judging him by what another man had done? "I'm sorry your father wasn't there when you needed him. I'm especially sorry because you're still paying for it, and so am I. What do I have to do to make you realize I'm not like him?"

"I invited you to come with me today, didn't I?"

"It isn't enough!" He knew his best hope of winning Daisy was to keep the conversation low-key. But it was in Chance's nature to fight for what he wanted. "I want to be with you every day, to see the changes as the baby grows. Already I noticed you're having trouble getting into the sports car."

"You think I'm fat?"

"No!" he said. "I think I need to trade this car in for a more practical one."

They reached the doctor's office parking lot, and there was no time for further discussion. Chance hoped his outburst hadn't scared her off.

He wasn't going to let Daisy get away. But he couldn't force her to back down, either.

It was enough to make a man's blood pressure shoot through the roof.

DAISY WAS GLAD when Chance caught her elbow and helped her out of the car. It really was too low. And he was so strong, and the fabric of his suit felt reassuringly sturdy against her bare arm.

She craved even more of his touch. She'd missed Chance all month, dreamed of him, relived their night together. Yet much as she longed to see him, she'd forced herself not to get her hopes up.

Had he been telling the truth about selling this playboy's dream of a car because of her and the baby? More likely that had been an easy promise that wouldn't be kept.

Chance held the heavy glass door of the medical building and escorted her to the elevator. When it opened, a couple stepped out, the woman seven or eight months pregnant, the man beaming with pride. They wore matched wedding rings, Daisy noticed.

A pang of envy wrenched her. What would it be like to have a real husband, a man who married her for love, not obligation? To be Chance's wife, really and truly.

No doubt she was so emotional because of pregnancy-related hormones, she told herself. It would pass.

In the doctor's office, the young receptionist took an admiring look at Chance while Daisy was signing in. No wonder. With his muscular build and strong jawline, he was the stuff of which female fantasies were made.

Chance didn't seem to notice the attention he aroused. But then, he was probably used to it.

They waited a few minutes before being called into an examining room where a large monitor and portable ultrasound equipment had been set up. The nurse left after instructing Daisy to change into a hospital-type gown.

Discreetly, Chance looked away. Even so, having him nearby made her nervous. Her cheeks heated when the wrapper-style gown parted thigh high as she climbed onto the examining table, and she tugged the front panels in dismay.

"Let me help." Chance's strong hands shifted her to a better position. "Comfortable?"

"I don't think I'm going to be comfortable for another six months," Daisy admitted. "I can't believe I'm this awkward so early."

"My sister Gigi claims she was mistaken for a whale when she was six months pregnant," he said. "But what could be more beautiful than a woman who's becoming a mother?"

"That sounds good," she said.

"You don't think I mean it?"

"According to Elise, your silver tongue is legendary."

"She must have been referring to my courtroom proficiency." He turned at a knock on the door. A second later in came Dr. Adhuri.

The slim, graying doctor shook hands with them both. "I'm pleased to meet you," he said to Chance. "This ultrasound is an important moment for many couples, which is why I prefer to perform it myself rather than using a technician."

"I appreciate that," Chance said.

He took Daisy's hand as the doctor parted the gown and squirted a gooey substance on her bare abdomen. Although only three months along, she could feel a new firmness in that part of her body.

With the sensing device, the doctor made light circles in the goo. On the adjacent TV monitor flashed blurry black and white images. Daisy wasn't sure how anyone could make out details.

Then she spotted a round shape that might be a head. Below it lay a small body with a pulse throbbing inside.

"That's your baby's heart beating," said Dr. Adhuri.

Chance's grip tightened on her hand. When she sneaked a peak at him, Daisy was startled to see tears in his eyes.

THE SIGHT OF HIS CHILD filled Chance with wonder. When he'd viewed prints of ultrasounds of his nieces and nephews, the images had intrigued him. This visceral thrill, however, carried him to a different dimension.

He and Daisy had created this life. They hadn't meant to, but could it have been entirely an accident?

"Look how perfect the baby is," he said. "Even before we knew it existed, it was growing and taking shape."

"Can the baby feel the pressure of the ultrasound equipment?" Daisy asked the doctor. "Can it hear our voices?"

"It's wiggling, so I'd say it's aware of us," said Dr. Adhuri. "As for hearing us, we know that by the time they're born, babies recognize their parents' voices."

"I was taking hormones before I found out I was pregnant," she said. "Did that create any problems?"

"Everything looks fine." The doctor pointed out the little arms and legs. "Would you like me to try to determine the sex? It isn't always possible, but sometimes we can see a male organ."

"That would be intruding on its privacy," Daisy said.

Chance agreed. "We don't need to know everything in advance."

"Then let's take photographs." The doctor selected a view and pressed a button, then repeated the process from several angles. After the pictures emerged photocopy-style from the equipment, he handed one to Daisy. "Here's the start of your scrapbook."

The shot, Chance saw, provided a profile glimpse. "Look at that little nose!" he said. "And the mouth. I think he's smiling. Is that possible?"

"It does look that way." The doctor beamed. Clearly he enjoyed this aspect of his work. It was enough to make Chance almost wish he'd become an obstetrician instead of an attorney.

After wiping the goo off Daisy's stomach, Dr. Adhuri departed. While she dressed, Chance kept peering at the print. It wasn't as thrilling as watching the baby flex its little hands and curl up in real time, but it still amazed him.

In six months he would be able to touch that nose and peer into those eyes in person. He could hardly wait.

"When are you due?" He counted the months in his head. "Let's see, that would be January. A New Year's baby!"

"I can't believe you're as excited as I am." Daisy regarded him thoughtfully as she brushed her hair.

Excited. And concerned. And keenly aware of his own precarious position, Chance realized.

He might be the father but he wasn't her husband. If she wanted, she could keep him at bay.

The law might give him certain rights, but to exercise them would alienate her. "Please don't shut me out," he said.

Daisy dropped the brush into her purse and clasped her hands in front of her linen dress. "I have an idea," she said. "But I don't know if you're going to like it."

"Try me," he said.

No ONE COULD MISTAKE the love shining in Chance's face as he'd watched their baby on the monitor. The man had bonded with the child. Daisy knew she couldn't keep these two apart.

"You can stay in my spare bedroom a couple of nights a week," she said. "I don't need to be taken care of, but it'll give you a chance to observe the changes in me as the baby grows. And we can discuss names and things like that."

Chance took a pocket organizer from his coat. "Tuesdays, Thursdays and Saturdays," he said. "How does that sound?"

"Fine. You aren't going to argue?" she asked.

"About what?"

"Because I'm not moving into your place."

He tapped in a notation and put the organizer away. "I'm willing to be flexible."

To Daisy's surprise, disappointment tugged at her. She'd assumed he would continue to press for marriage, or at least for full-time cohabitation. The fact that he'd given up easily proved that his heart hadn't really been in it.

"Now what?" Chance said. "You're getting your way, but you don't look happy about it."

"It's nothing." Daisy straightened her dress. "I'd better go make my next appointment."

"When do we start childbirth classes?"

"Not until after your sister's wedding, I hope!" She couldn't handle too many demands on her at one time.

"Besides, I'm sure I'll forget how to huff and puff if we start too early."

"Whenever you say," he responded. "Today's Monday, so that means I can bring my stuff over tomorrow. Why don't we plan on eating dinner together?"

"If I'm cooking, we're eating frozen food," she said.

"I'm cooking."

"You're on." She wondered if she'd made a mistake, inviting him to stay over at her house three nights a week. But it was too late to back out now. Besides, she realized she liked the thought of playing house with Chance, on her terms.

Chapter Nine

On Monday evening Daisy surveyed her condo as if mentally preparing for an invasion. Which, in a way, she was.

Would Chance move the couch closer to the TV? Would he eat snacks in the living room and drop crumbs on the carpet? If he'd struck her as bossy in the past, what would he be like when he had his own key and the right to come and go?

This wasn't the sort of topic Daisy felt comfortable broaching to her friends. What she needed was some objective advice.

In the kitchen, she took out her copy of *2001 Ways to Wed*. She vaguely recalled seeing something in Jane Jasmine's book about living together.

As her hot chocolate heated in the microwave, Daisy sat at the table and flipped through the pages. "First Impressions, And How to Make Them Work For You."

She didn't need that chapter, she thought wryly. She'd made quite a first impression on Chance, one that was going to last a lifetime.

"Warning Signs: Avoiding Abuse Before It Starts." Although she doubted Elise's brother had caveman tendencies, she ran through the warning signs for good measure. Jealousy. Enforced isolation. A torrent of gifts, as if the man were trying to buy her. A demand that she account for every minute of her day. None of those points applied, thank goodness.

When the microwave timer rang, Daisy fetched the chocolate drink. It provided lots of calcium, and it tasted good, too.

She returned to her reading.

"Physical Imperfections and Why They Shouldn't Make a Difference." Oh, lovely! According to Jane Jasmine, putting on a few pounds wasn't a cardinal sin. Of course, she probably hadn't had this particular kind of weight gain in mind, Daisy mused.

"Living Together." The chapter heading didn't reveal much, so she read the first few paragraphs.

Some people consider cohabitation to be a good way to find out if they're marriage compatible, but studies show otherwise. In fact, living together predicts almost nothing about marriage. After all, you haven't made a commitment. And you're not dealing with such key issues as finances, in-laws and children.

Daisy wrinkled her nose. Obviously, it hadn't occurred to Jane Jasmine that a woman who made a certain kind of first impression might have to deal with all of those issues, whether she wanted to or not.

The doorbell rang. When Daisy answered it, she was surprised to see Chance in the hall.

"I thought you said Tuesdays, Thursdays and Saturdays," she blurted. "It's Monday."

He grinned. "I'm glad to see you, too."

She hadn't been very gracious, had she? "I'm sorry," Daisy said.

"I want to show you something. Downstairs." Chance had removed his tie and jacket after work, and he looked so appealingly rumpled that Daisy got an itch to muss his hair and unbutton his shirt.

Just to tease him. Just to see if he would respond by clasping her around the waist and bringing his mouth down to hers.

Oh, right!

"What is it?" she asked as she grabbed her purse and keys.

"See for yourself." Merriment danced in his eyes.

As they went downstairs, Daisy wondered what he'd brought. Baby furniture? Theme decorations? After his response to the ultrasound, he might have gone overboard.

"You don't have to buy me anything," she said.

"Don't worry. I didn't." He chuckled until she wanted to smack him.

"You can be downright maddening, you know that?" Daisy grumped.

"That's what the opposing attorneys always say," he responded.

They entered the lobby at the same time as Jeff Hawkin appeared from the pool area. He spent so many hours at Mesa Blue, Daisy would have believed he lived there if she hadn't been told otherwise.

"If you're going out tonight, you should come by The Prickly Pear," said the handyman, who doubled as a bartender at the restaurant. "It's going to be interesting."

"What's going on?" Daisy asked.

When the young man grinned, his teeth were startlingly white against his deep tan. "I promised to make Frannie one of my special fruit-drink concoctions, and I reminded Bill that we have free snacks on Monday nights."

"You're setting them up to run into each other?" Chance said.

"Just trying to get them together again." Jeff winked. "Hey, everybody needs somebody, right? Besides, I work with Bill, and it's hard on me when he's so miserable."

"That's sweet." Daisy wondered when Jeff was going to find himself a girlfriend. But then, the way young women hung around him, there was no hurry for him to settle down.

As she stepped out of the lobby, cool air raised goose bumps along Daisy's arms. She folded her arms in front of her for warmth. It had been so hot today that when she got home she'd thrown on shorts and a sleeveless blouse, but the nights chilled rapidly in a desert climate.

"You can wear my jacket. It's in the car." Chance opened a maroon luxury sedan by the curb.

"This isn't your car," Daisy said.

"It is now."

She couldn't believe it. "You did this because of the baby?" she said. "It's only been a couple of hours."

"Get in," Chance said. "I'll take you for a spin."

He helped her into the passenger seat. "It's a lot easier than getting into the sports car," she admitted.

"That's the idea." He came around to the other side.

Daisy couldn't shake the sense that she was sitting in a stranger's car. "If you were a teenager, I'd think you stole it."

Sliding behind the steering wheel, Chance laughed.

"Believe me, my bank account says otherwise." He started the engine.

"You really got rid of the sports car?" Daisy asked.

They glided away from the curb, almost floating along the pavement. "Yes," Chance said. "To be honest, I'd been thinking about getting a more practical car. I'm thirty-five, after all."

"One foot in the grave," she teased.

"One foot in parenthood," he amended. "There's a built-in child seat in back. A computer guidance device in case I get lost. And you should hear the CD system!"

"*Now* I believe you bought it." It made sense that he'd found an even better toy. Still, this afternoon's ultrasound had clearly influenced his decision. "I'm still having trouble believing you gave up the sports car."

"Don't underestimate my commitment," he said.

They swooped through the quiet streets. Chance demonstrated how smoothly the car cornered, how easily it stopped and how quickly it accelerated. At last they skimmed to a halt in The Prickly Pear's parking lot.

"You're curious to see what happens with Frannie and Bill?" Daisy asked.

"That, and this place has free snacks on Monday night. After what I spent on these wheels, I need all the help I can get," he joked.

After they got out, Chance draped his suit jacket over Daisy's shoulders. Warmth and his spicy fragrance enveloped her. When his arm looped around her waist, she grew even warmer.

As they walked, he matched his pace to hers, despite

his long legs. Maybe, like her, he was in no hurry to end their solitude.

Daisy glanced up at the skyful of stars. Even the city glare didn't erase their brightness, especially when she was with Chance.

They reached a shadowed patch of sidewalk, a few paces shy of the light spilling through the restaurant's front window. He brushed his lips across Daisy's forehead and drew her close.

He cradled her against him, and she reveled in his hard, reassuring presence and the gentleness of his embrace. Starfires tingled across her skin.

Footsteps slapped toward them. "None of that!" declared Elise's voice. "You two have to set a good example for the baby."

Reluctantly lifting her head, Daisy saw her friend approaching on James's arm. "Did Jeff tell you to come, too?"

She nodded. "Too bad Phoebe and Wyatt promised to have dinner with the Madisons. They're missing a major episode in the soap opera of Frannie and Bill."

"She's assuming the two stars of our show will show up," James added. 'I'm far from confident."

They went into the restaurant. At this late dinner hour, the tables and booths were filled with couples and small families.

Jeff waved from the horseshoe-shaped bar. "Help yourselves." He indicated a minibuffet of hors d'oeuvres. There was no sign of Frannie or Bill.

The men filled their plates with nacho chips and ordered drinks. Elise chose vegetables with a little dip. Now that she'd bought her wedding gown, she was being careful not to gain weight.

As usual these days, Daisy's appetite was big enough

for two. She took a sample of everything on the buffet, then ordered a nonalcoholic drink.

"We had our first counseling session this afternoon," James announced when they were all seated around the curved end of the bar.

"I like the therapist." To Daisy Elise explained, "Her name's Beatrice, like Dante's heroine. I enjoy classical references."

"Don't tell me you plan to name our kids Aphrodite and Apollo!" James said in mock horror.

"We'll deal with that at a later session," his bride-to-be returned.

"What exactly happens in counseling, anyway?" Daisy asked.

Peripherally she saw Frannie enter. Her garish red hair quivered as she approached, then sat within earshot of the little group.

"We talked about our expectations," Elise said. "What our concerns are and how we plan to handle key issues."

"It never occurred to me that every family is a kind of subculture of its own," James admitted. "We expect when we get married that our new family will act like the one we came from, whether that means everyone sitting down to meals together or everyone eating helter-skelter."

"People getting married are like immigrants from two different countries," Elise explained. "We can't assume that there's only one right way of handling finances or planning for the future. Or of picking what TV program to watch, either. We have to discuss things."

Frannie's gaze shot toward the door and then she looked quickly away. A moment later Bill took a seat on the far side of the horseshoe bar. Jeff bustled around, fixing his special drinks.

Daisy decided she might as well break the latest news. "Chance is going to stay with me three nights a week. He wants to be close to the baby."

"We saw the ultrasound today," he added. "It was astounding! I can't tell you...well, you'll find out for yourselves, one of these days."

"I never had children," said Frannie, joining the conversation. "You're a lucky girl, Daisy, even if you're not married."

"Thanks." Her heart went out to her lonely neighbor.

"To some people, cats are like children," Bill said from the far side of the bar. The large man tasted his drink, which was topped with a pineapple chunk and a cherry.

"Is that a criticism?" Frannie drummed her many-ringed fingers on the bar.

"Not at all," he said. "I never appreciated cats until I started watching yours. Each one has its own personality, doesn't it? And they seem very attached to you."

The cat lady's expression softened. "I wish I could rescue every stray in Phoenix."

Bill cleared his throat, as if gathering courage to take the next step. Then he removed a folded newspaper clipping from his jacket. "I happened to run across this. It's about a group that helps wild cat colonies."

"Help them in what way?" Frannie asked.

"They trap them, get them spayed or neutered, then return them to the colony and feed them." He held it out like a peace offering.

Jeff could have taken the clipping and passed it across the horseshoe bar, but he suddenly got very busy polishing glasses. Unable to resist the bait, Frannie carried her drink around to Bill. "Let me see that."

Elise hid a delighted smile behind her hand. Daisy felt a little guilty, spying on this bashful romance, but she was glad Bill had taken the initiative. Since his hobbies were camping, fishing and watching hockey games, he'd obviously gone to some pains to please Frannie.

"Are you going to get counseling?" James asked.

"Excuse me?" she said.

"You and Chance. The two of you must have a lot to negotiate concerning the baby," he prompted. "Co-parenting and all that."

"Sounds like a good idea," Chance said. "Daisy?"

"We have nothing to negotiate," she answered coolly. "This isn't a democracy."

"You're setting yourself up as a dictator?" he teased.

"You'd better believe it."

His mouth quirked in amusement. "For a guy who likes to run things his own way, I sure tangled with the wrong woman."

"You like strong women," she countered. "I mean, I assume you do. After all, you were once—I mean, your former—" Too late she realized that his broken engagement might be a touchy subject.

"You mean Gillian?" he said. "She was a pushover compared to you."

"She ate nails for breakfast," Elise corrected. "But she put sugar on them."

A few seats away, Bill and Frannie were loudly discussing joining a group to rescue wild cats. The way they kept staring into each other's eyes, however, they probably wouldn't have noticed if a cheetah, two lions and a tiger had strolled through The Prickly Pear.

"Gillian had an iron fist in a velvet glove?" James queried.

"Iron fist giving him the finger and disappearing to points east," Elise said.

"We parted on good terms," Chance said. "But you're right, Daisy. I do like strong women. I particularly like you."

This statement of affection in front of his sister meant a lot, even if it fell short of a declaration of love.

Daisy intended to give her baby everything she'd lacked, including a sense of belonging to a family. And she was beginning to believe, despite her wariness, that Chance might be the right man to help her.

AFTER WORK ON Tuesday Chance stopped by a florist's shop and picked out a bouquet of daisies and pink roses. They reminded him of his Deirdre.

His Deirdre.

He wasn't sure she was his, or ever would be, that was the problem. For one thing he'd noticed in the restaurant last night how men kept turning to stare at her.

And no wonder. She was radiant. Picky or not, she must have plenty of admirers.

She could also be maddeningly stubborn. The ideal woman that Chance had formulated in his mind would meet him halfway, not keep demanding that he prove himself. She would see the logic of his plans and disagree only when she had a rational reason for doing so.

It was strange, though, how the image of that ideal woman kept fading like a distant radio signal. He was too busy wondering whether, on being handed a bouquet, Daisy would chirp with delight or throw it in his face.

As it turned out, she did neither. She accepted the flowers with thanks and went to put them in a vase, leaving Chance to lug in his overnight bag and a large suitcase filled with layette items donated by his sisters.

They'd surprised him with the haul after church on Sunday. In addition they offered to provide the curtains for the baby's room, a diaper stacker, crib, bassinet, comforters, sheets, a swing, bounce chair and stroller. He didn't want to bring over too many items, though, because he still hoped Daisy would move into his house.

"You don't travel light, do you?" She returned from the kitchen with the flowers in a green vase. As she set it on the coffee table, she turned it until Chance saw with a jolt that the pot had a face. His face.

A caricature of his face, actually. Slashing black eyebrows. Leering, oversize eyes. An oily grin. All it lacked was a villainous mustache.

"I was mad at you when I made this," she said. "I told you while it was firing that I would give it you, but when I saw it again, I decided it was too extreme. I'll make you another one."

"It's a—what did you call it?—a Personality Pot," he recalled, embarrassed that, with so much on his mind, he'd forgotten the works in her studio. "If I weren't the one getting skewered, I'd find it delightful."

Daisy took a deep breath. "I've made a couple of dozen this month. I think they're getting better. More skillful and more original."

"What are you going to do with them?" He dropped his luggage by the couch.

"I don't know." As she bent to sniff the flowers, her auburn hair swung smoothly forward. "I might stick a couple in the sales gallery and see if anyone buys them."

"You ought to stage your own show." He made himself comfortable on the couch. As comfortable as he could be while facing that unflattering image of himself. "Give yourself an opening night and invite the critics."

Daisy hugged herself protectively. "No way!"

Instead of debating, Chance asked, "How do you see yourself? Primarily, I mean. As a gallery owner or as an artist?"

"I never thought about it." She dropped onto the couch beside him. "I'd never give up the gallery, but being an artist is an essential part of who I am."

"What about the baby?" He hadn't meant to change the subject, but her comment brought the inevitable reality into focus. "How are you going to juggle your busy schedule with motherhood?"

She stretched her legs in their jeans. Chance would have preferred a more revealing top than her tucked-in camp shirt, but it did have a low vee neckline.

Besides, Daisy looked cute in almost anything. And even cuter, he recalled, in nothing.

"I'll find a baby-sitter," she said.

As his wife, Daisy could afford to work part-time and hire more help at the gallery, but Chance doubted she would appreciate the suggestion. She would probably put it into the category of "efforts to run her life."

"I can watch the baby on Saturdays," he offered.

"You're willing to change diapers?"

"I've got seven younger sisters. I've changed plenty in my time. And heated bottles, put Band-Aids on boo-boos and shoveled in the baby food," he said.

"Amazing."

"Not really."

"You're right. Women do it all the time. So you don't think I'll make a fool of myself, displaying my pots in the sales gallery?" Daisy said, returning to what was obviously a more pressing concern.

At least she was asking his advice instead of rejecting it. "I find your work—well, I'm not good with adjectives. But I'd buy one for my house, even if I didn't know you."

"That's good to hear." Smiling, Daisy curled on the couch a few inches from him.

It took a lot of restraint not to make a move, because from this angle the open vee neckline of her camp shirt revealed the swelling tops of her breasts and a wisp of pink lace from her bra. Chance remembered in luscious detail how soft those breasts were in his hands, and how the nipples sprang erect beneath his lips.

"I hope other people like them as much as you do." Daisy's comment gave him a jolt, until Chance realized she was talking about her vases. "I haven't decided how much to charge for them."

"Shakira gets thousands of dollars for a painting," he pointed out. "Do you put as much time into one piece as she does?"

"People won't pay as much for pottery as for paintings and sculptures, regardless of how much time is involved," she said. "I'll start at five hundred dollars a pot, and see if any of them sell."

"At least you won't have to pay a commission to a gallery owner," he said. "Since you own the place."

"True." She leaned back, and as he ruffled his fingers through her hair, her eyelids drifted shut. "That feels good. A little too good."

"How can anything feel too good?" He massaged her scalp with his fingertips. "That reminds me, I promised you back rubs, didn't I?"

With obvious reluctance, Daisy sat up. "I can't tell you how hard it is to refuse your offer, but we both know it's too risky to start touching each other."

"Why? I can't get you pregnant," he shot back.

Mischievously she poked him in the side. "That wasn't a very seductive line! What happened to the fabled playboy charm I've heard so much about?"

Chance's hand darted in and mussed her hair, treating her the way he would one of his sisters. "I'm supposed to be a playboy, am I?"

"I have it on the best authority." She landed a light blow to the shoulder.

"From Elise, right?" Scooting forward, he caught Daisy's arm and pulled her flat on the couch behind him. "Don't believe everything you hear." He yanked up her shirt, bent and blew on her bare stomach.

"Hey, stop that!" Giggling, she tried to brush him away.

"I'm making music for the baby." He blew on her again.

"That isn't exactly Mozart!"

"Mozart is highly overrated." He sat up. "You see? Having me around is a barrel of laughs."

"I wish I had a videotape to show your lawyer friends what you're really like." Her cheeks bright pink, Daisy wriggled away and tucked in her shirt.

It surprised Chance that he'd treated the future mother of his child the way he might have treated his sisters Gigi or Sharon or Elise when they were younger. But what was wrong with a little playfulness? If two people were going to spend time together, they ought to be able to have innocent fun once in a while.

Innocent. Well, not entirely. The contact had aroused him and, he hoped, her as well. The next logical step would be to scoop this lady in his arms and carry her to an even more private place.

"No," Daisy said.

"No to what?"

"To whatever you're planning. You're breathing hard, and your pupils are enlarged," she said. "I'll show you the spare bedroom."

Hopping to her feet, she grabbed his overnight bag and started down the hallway.

How could she withdraw at a time like this? She'd been breathing hard, too, Chance could have sworn. The woman must have nerves of steel.

He took the larger suitcase and followed her. "Are we sharing a bathroom?"

"You can use the guest powder room," she said. "It's got a shower, no tub. I hope you don't leave towels on the floor. Also, please make me a list of snacks you like so I can stock them."

"You don't have to do that."

"Yes, I do. Otherwise you'll eat up my favorite snacks, and these days, I need all the food I can get."

"Good point."

Daisy directed him to a bedroom decorated in the same low-key style as the rest of the condo. "That's the kind of agreeable attitude I like."

"I'll remember that." Chance dropped the suitcase inside the door.

"Sleep well," she said, and hurried away.

Left alone, he gazed around with the dismay of a tomcat plopped into a cage at the animal shelter. The surroundings might be comfortable, but the situation left a lot to be desired.

A lot to be desired. That was the problem, precisely.

Chapter Ten

During the next month, Daisy slept soundly, thanks to her pregnancy hormones. Her waking moments, however, resonated with Chance's nearness.

Once, at breakfast, his robe gaped open to reveal a broad chest with a sprinkling of light-brown hair. Another time he left the bathroom door ajar while brushing his teeth, and she glimpsed his gleaming, shirtless torso. And then there was the longing in his gray eyes each time they separated in the evening.

Daisy's yearning to touch him smoldered like fire. Especially now that the endometriosis no longer bothered her, only her busy schedule and rigid self-control kept the flames banked.

It would be so easy to solve this problem by going to bed with him. And such a terrible mistake. Daisy would be handing her heart to a man who could never be tamed.

One morning downtown she spotted him striding toward the Civic Plaza, wearing his suit like armor and wielding his briefcase like a weapon. En route to the courthouse, he was a knight on his way to do battle, eyes hard, jaw tight.

The image thrilled and unsettled her. Daisy sensed

that Chance needed a different sort of woman, someone who belonged with him in every way. Someone like Gillian, a fellow attorney who surely had understood him better than Daisy could ever hope to.

She didn't know how to love Chance halfway. For her, it would be heart and soul. But not for him.

She didn't dare try. If she did and lost him, the pain would be unbearable.

One Saturday evening in mid-August, the two of them ate a light supper and went for a swim. The water of the blue-tiled pool provided a welcome relief after the searing heat of the day.

Daisy kept trying not to stare at Chance's muscular body, boldly revealed by his slim black trunks. As he sheared through the water, his corded thighs and back muscles rippled alluringly.

She needed to find an activity for tonight that would distract them both. Chance had asked her to go dancing and, when she nixed that, had offered to show her how his new artwork, including the Personality Pot she'd given him, looked in his house.

Oh, sure, Daisy thought ruefully. That was the worst possible way to spend this evening, sequestered in the very place where they'd become lovers. The result would be a foregone conclusion.

Neither Elise nor Phoebe was likely to provide any help. Both were wrapped up in their happily-ever-after love affairs. Elise was wholly involved in planning her September wedding, and Phoebe, becoming more impatient as time went by, had scheduled hers for October.

"Hey! You swimming or daydreaming?" Chance challenged, arcing past her on his umpteenth lap. He worked out regularly, she'd learned, lifting weights at home, jogging and, now that he was spending three nights a week with her, swimming.

Daisy continued dog-paddling in the deep end. "I'm indulging in an artist's reverie," she said.

"Another creative idea?" His voice drifted back as he cut through the water.

That reminded Daisy that she had something to tell him. Before she could, she saw Helen and Rolland Madison stroll into the courtyard. The elderly couple went for a walk nearly every evening.

They stopped near Daisy. "I don't suppose you've talked to Frannie today, have you?" Helen asked.

"I'm afraid not." Frannie and Bill had stayed on friendly terms with each other these past few weeks, but she hadn't seen either of them recently.

"Well, she and Bill are up to something," Helen said. "I don't think it could be dangerous..."

"I'm sure they'll be fine," soothed her husband.

"You know how scattered she can be," Helen went on. "Bill's a good influence, but a man in love isn't always sensible."

Daisy lifted herself from the pool and sat dripping on the rim. "What can I do to help?"

"I wish someone responsible would keep an eye on them tonight," her neighbor said. "If my arthritis weren't acting up, I'd do it myself."

"Helen! We don't want to impose," cautioned Rolland. "I'm sure these young people have other plans."

"No, we don't," Daisy said. Any idea that would keep her and Chance too busy to get intimate would be welcome.

Chance swam up. "Hi, folks. What's going on?"

"My wife is worried about Frannie and Bill," said

the former Navy man, standing with feet apart, his back ramrod straight.

"They're going out tonight with a couple of new friends," Helen explained. "Helping a cat colony, Frannie said. Does that sound safe to you? I mean, a colony!"

"I doubt the cats carry muskets, dear," Rolland said dryly.

"What if Frannie gets scratched or bitten?" his wife went on. "Cats can carry rabies, can't they?"

"Now you've got me curious," Chance admitted. "I'd like to see what they're doing."

"You're an attorney," Helen said. "At least I'd know that if they get arrested, they'll get good advice."

"Arrested for what?" Daisy asked.

"Who knows?" said her neighbor. "Maybe they're sneaking onto other people's property."

"We'll look into it," Chance said. "What time are they leaving?"

"After dinner, according to Frannie," Rolland said. "That could mean now."

Chance joined Daisy on the concrete. "We'll get dressed and go talk to her." He grabbed his towel.

After thanking them, the Madisons continued on their walk. Daisy dried off, self-conscious beneath Chance's gaze.

"By the way, I hope it's all right with you," he said. "I volunteered us without thinking."

"It's a bit late to ask now." She smiled. "But that's okay. I'm curious, too."

"DON'T TOUCH ANY of the cats," Frannie warned Daisy as they stood amid a small cluster of people near a large apartment complex. "You're pregnant, and cats can carry—what's it called, that disease that causes birth defects?''

''Toxoplasmosis,'' said Nell Beecham.

Chance was still absorbing the discovery that his grandmotherly secretary was, in private life, a cat rescuer. Both of her Siamese had been adopted from shelters, and, she'd explained a few minutes ago, she'd been involved in saving feral, or wild-born, cats for the past year.

Their group consisted of him and Daisy, Bill and Frannie, Nell and her friend Sarita, also in her sixties. Tonight's mission involved returning a newly neutered male cat, unhappily residing in a large carrier, to his stomping grounds.

In addition, Frannie had explained, they would feed the cats and watch for any new arrivals. By trapping the animals, getting them fixed and giving them vaccines, the group kept the cats healthy and prevented the breeding, yowling, fighting and trash-can destruction that offended neighbors.

''Cats are creatures of habit,'' Nell said as they walked toward a nearby alley. ''They form colonies where there's food. In this case people leave trash behind the apartments, even though there are closed containers available.''

''We got the landlord's permission before we started our work,'' added Sarita, a tall woman with dramatically white-streaked black hair. Like the other three rescuers, she wore long pants, a long-sleeved jacket and gloves for protection.

''We explained to the neighbors how our system works to their advantage,'' Nell said. They entered the alley at a slow pace, keeping their voices low so as not to frighten the cats. Ahead, Chance heard some mewing, but he couldn't see any animals in the semidarkness.

"What advantage?" Daisy asked. "I mean, I admire what you're doing, but don't most people want the animals trapped and taken away?"

"If you remove the colony," Nell said as crisply as if giving instructions to their paralegal service, "new cats will be attracted by the trash. They will breed like crazy, and soon you've got a bunch more. This way, the colony remains stable and trouble free."

"How long do you keep feeding them?" Chance asked.

"For the rest of their lives. We care about these animals or we wouldn't be here." Tonight his secretary was in charge, as her tone made clear.

He didn't mind. In fact, he didn't notice much difference in her behavior tonight from the way she ran his office.

The meowing got louder. Chance noted several distinctive voices, some screechier, some softer. "Can't any of them be tamed and adopted?"

Frannie sighed. "I saw the cutest tortoiseshell the other night. He came over and circled me a couple of times."

"Stray cats that used to belong to people often can be tamed," Sarita said. "The ones born wild usually can't."

"Look!" Daisy, walking a few steps ahead, stopped in her tracks. "There they are!"

Beyond her, Chance saw rapid movements in the twilight. A tail disappeared behind a trash can. A ginger kitty face peered from inside a cardboard box.

Other, bolder cats paced toward them, although none came within grabbing distance. Not that any person in his right mind would grab a feral cat. It didn't take much imagination to picture the clawing, hissing and biting that would result.

A little awkwardly, Bill and Frannie went to work under Sarita's direction. They set out metal bowls, filling most with dry cat food and a few with water from a jug.

Nell lowered the carrier to the pavement and crouched. She talked in a soothing voice to the creature inside before opening the door. Then she stepped away.

Around them, cats swarmed to their dinner. Chance counted at least a dozen, ranging from Chihuahua size to one nearly as big as a cocker spaniel.

Varying stripes and splotches of color distinguished the animals. One was mostly black and another white except for its raccoon-striped tail.

"They've each got a special personality," Nell told him. "After a while you get to know them."

"They're so cute!" Daisy was watching with the glee of a child at Christmas.

"I wish I could take them all home with me," Frannie said.

"Not these cats," Nell warned.

One animal, furred with black, orange and cream patches, approached Frannie. Chance thought it was going to rub her ankles, but it mewed a couple of times and withdrew.

"That one's a stray," Sarita said. "Judging by his behavior, he must have been a pet at one time."

"He's lonely," Frannie said.

"Do you suppose we could take him with us?" Bill asked. "If not tonight, then another time?"

"It depends on how friendly he gets," Nell said. "Even if you manage to get him home, he might come running back to his usual haunts unless you keep him inside.''

"Inside?" Bill swallowed hard. "He'd wreck my place."

"I could work with him," Frannie said. "Cats can be trained, if you're patient."

"What the heck," said her boyfriend. "Who needs decor, anyway?"

"Here he comes." Sarita indicated the open carrier containing the newly neutered male.

From inside crept a tan-striped cat. Ears flattened, he peered around, sniffed the air and then raced for the cover of a row of trash cans.

"We'll leave the food and come back for the bowls later. We've got two more colonies to feed tonight." Nell went to collect the carrier.

As they walked back through the alley, Bill fell into place next to Chance, behind the women. The condo superintendent cleared his throat.

"I've never been much of a cat person," he admitted. "They are interesting, though."

"They certainly are," Chance said, although what he'd enjoyed most was watching Daisy's delight in the colony.

"Sometimes, when you're crazy about someone, you have to let the woman lead the way and follow her," Bill said.

"What do you mean?"

"I'm an outdoorsman, myself, and when I can't go camping, I like to take in a ball game. But cats are Frannie's thing, so I'd better make them my thing, too. Of course, she has to meet me halfway, but I'm sure she will."

You have to let the woman lead the way. That was worth thinking about, Chance conceded.

When Daisy was tucked into his luxury sedan, he drove away slowly, not heading anywhere in particular. "Did you have fun tonight?"

Moonlight turned her eyes a haunting silver-green. "I think it's great to be able to help someone, whether it's a person or an animal. What these rescuers are doing, you can see the results right in front of you."

"The cats don't exactly run over and thank you for helping them."

"People don't always do that, either."

"True," he said. "Hey, I wanted to ask you a question. About our relationship."

She stiffened. "Yes?"

"You said once that I'm too bossy."

"Did I?"

"Do you still think so?" he asked. "Bill said tonight that it's important to follow the woman's lead once in a while. I was wondering if I do that enough."

Daisy stared down at her lap. "I don't know."

"Come on, you have an opinion about everything else," Chance teased.

"It's a weird thing to be talking about," she said.

"Why?"

Daisy's chest rose and fell in agitation. "I don't know how to have this kind of discussion. It isn't the way people talk, in my experience."

"How do they talk?" he asked, stopping at a red light. He'd instinctively driven toward his office, now only a few blocks away.

"They talk about experiences they've had," Daisy said, "and people they know, movies they've seen, politics, stuff like that. Or they fight and call each other names. But they don't discuss...don't discuss... whatever it is we're discussing.''

''The balance of power in our relationship,'' he said.

''I don't know what that means.''

Like a lot of people, she'd never learned the fine points of intimate communication. Chance only knew as much as he did because, years ago, he and Gillian had undergone premarital counseling in an unsuccessful attempt to prevent their careers from pulling them apart.

He cared about Daisy, and he found himself wanting to educate her. Which, he admitted silently, was downright arrogant of him.

''It means we have to treat each other with respect,'' he said simply, ''so both of us get what we need.''

''Oh!'' She gave an excited little bounce. ''I nearly forgot to tell you something. In fact, I could use your advice. Would you mind stopping at my gallery?''

''I'd be glad to.'' As for communicating, he supposed they'd done enough for one evening, at least on the verbal level.

Native Art was dark at this hour. They entered through the back, by the eerie glow of safety lights.

Daisy shepherded him to the sales gallery, where she switched on the overhead fixture. ''There!'' Triumphantly she pointed to an empty space between a desertscape and a playful metal armadillo.

''You brought me here to show me a blank spot?'' Chance teased. ''Wait! It's some kind of—what do they call it?—performance art, right? We stand here and after a while we notice the contours of the empty space. Then we admire the dust motes.''

Daisy smacked him on the arm. ''Don't be silly!

That's where my Personality Pot sat, the one that sold today. For five hundred dollars!''

Pride surged through him. He was even happier for her, Chance realized, than if he himself had scored a coup. ''Congratulations!''

''It was only on display for a week,'' she added.

He wrapped his arms around Daisy, big-brother style. Her bright wedge of hair brushed his cheek, yielding the scent of rose petals. In his embrace, she felt delicate and wonderfully rounded.

''I need your advice about which pot to replace it with,'' she murmured.

''A face that's as different as possible,'' he said against her hair. ''One of your customers who didn't buy the old one might prefer the new one.''

''Good strategy.'' She made no attempt to slip away.

Chance stroked her abdomen lightly. ''You're becoming more womanly every day.''

''Womanly?'' Daisy peered past him to a full-length mirror, angled to add depth to the small sales gallery. ''Clunky is more like it.''

''No way!'' Reflected in the glass, a loose-fitting sundress drifted across the contours of her body. She had gained weight in the middle, but what he noticed most was her glow. ''You look spectacular.''

''It bothers me when I see the magazine covers at the supermarket, displaying skinny women in bikinis,'' she admitted. ''I feel so roly-poly by comparison.''

''I like your roly-poly.'' With his arms around her, he massaged the length of her back. ''Skinny women may look good to a camera, but they're all bones when you hold them.''

''Held a lot, have you?'' Daisy replied, half-joking.

Obviously, she'd heard the vastly exaggerated rumors of his conquests. "A few," Chance said. "I like you much better."

He tipped up her chin and moved his mouth over hers, relishing her full lips and the hot tip of tongue that tantalized him. Bracing himself, he caught her bottom with one hand while fluffing back her hair and kissing her thoroughly.

Daisy tensed and tried to wriggle away. He held her firmly as he trailed kisses along her jawline and into the shell of her ear.

She gasped and caught his shoulder. After their swim, Chance had changed into a short-sleeved navy jersey that was like a second skin, and when she ran her hand across his chest, he might have been wearing nothing at all.

He didn't want anything between them. Not clothing, not inhibitions. Hard and hot, he would have taken her immediately had there been a couch handy.

"Daisy," Chance rasped, drawing her even closer. "Let's go...the nearest...your place. My office. I don't care."

"Oh, my gosh!" Her exclamation puzzled him.

"What?"

"I felt something move!" she said. "Inside. When you squished me against you."

"I didn't squish you!"

"Whatever. Right here." Easing away, she touched her small bulge. "Do you think it could be the baby moving? I'm only four months along."

"One of my sisters..." Chance stopped in midsentence. "To heck with my sisters! I want to feel it, too." He dropped to his knees, ignoring the hardness of the floor, and rested his cheek against the front of her dress.

Warmth radiated through the thin fabric. Inside, life

pulsated, but perhaps he was only detecting the natural rhythms of Daisy's body.

"Did you feel anything?" she asked.

"Your stomach's gurgling."

"It is not! Is it?"

"No." Reluctantly he stood up. "I'm not sure what was going on, but if you noticed movement, it must be real. Gee, should I have proposed again while I was down there?"

Daisy chuckled. "You're hopeless!"

The seductive mood had vanished. Reclaiming it was a lost cause, he decided.

"I think it's a boy," Chance said, to see how she would react. "In honor of tonight's outing, we should name him Tom."

She played along. "If it's a girl, how about Kitty?"

He struggled to come up with another boy's name. "I can't top that one. We're even."

"No, we're not. Allie," she said. "As in alley cat. I win."

"Okay, you get to name our first cat," he conceded.

"Sore loser!" She grinned. "Help me lug another Personality Pot out here and I'll forgive you."

The one she chose was a mischievous take on a sexy movie star, a woman whose beestung lips and extreme eyelashes generated both fervent admiration and gibes in the press about fooling Mother Nature. Chance helped remove it from the back room and install it in the sales gallery.

It was ironic, he reflected as they left. They hadn't made love and yet he felt closer to her tonight than ever before.

Chapter Eleven

There was too much silence coming from the kitchen.

Yawning her way out of the bathroom on Sunday morning, Daisy stood in the hallway and wondered why Chance wasn't clattering pans as usual. The man had a demonic energy in the morning, and on the weekend he often made French toast or pancakes.

She tightened the sash on her pale-green robe and padded across the living room. When she entered the kitchen, she caught sight of him at the table, reading a book.

A white trade-size paperback. With the name Jane Jasmine printed in blue letters on the front.

It hadn't occurred to Daisy that it was foolish to leave *2001 Ways to Wed* in plain sight, now that Chance was spending so much time here. She wished she'd buried it in her bookcase.

"Good morning." As she sauntered in, her stomach protested the scent of freshly brewed coffee. Reminding herself that she used to drink the stuff by the gallon, she plopped a teabag into a cup of water and stuck it in the microwave.

"This is ironic." Chance laid the book down. "A woman who cast my marriage proposal into the outer darkness turns out to be desperately seeking a husband.''

''I am not!'' Well, maybe she had been, but only because she wanted children and needed to start having them soon. ''Your sister and Phoebe bought that for me when they were matchmaking.''

Aloud, he read a chapter heading. '' 'Dressing For Success: Is There Such a Thing As Too Sexy?' Don't tell me you're letting this woman guide you through life!''

''That's one of the sillier chapters,'' Daisy protested. ''Most of it has solid psychological underpinnings.''

''Can I borrow it?'' he asked. ''In the law, we have a period called discovery in which both sides review each other's evidence. That helps us prepare our cases.''

''You want to plan your defense?''

He chuckled. ''Something like that.''

Daisy snatched the book from his hands. ''Buy your own copy.''

''And subsidize this kind of thing?'' He was only joking, though, because he added, ''Actually, I read several chapters and found them thought provoking.''

''Did you learn anything?'' When the timer dinged, Daisy stirred sugar into her tea and began toasting bread. She knew Chance had to leave soon to join his family at church.

One of these days she might go with him. She'd met a couple of his and Elise's younger sisters before and liked them.

But she wasn't ready to take such a step. It would be like a declaration of coupledom.

''I learned that I'm not abusive,'' Chance said. ''I learned that you made a terrific first impression. And I learned that you ought to marry me because living together isn't even close to the same thing.''

Was this more of his kidding? Not that Daisy doubted the sincerity of his proposal. But the two of them had little in common beyond having accidentally become parents-to-be.

Yet these past few weeks she'd become comfortable having Chance nearby. On the nights when he didn't stay over, she rattled around the condo at loose ends. As she probably would tonight.

''I like things the way they are,'' Daisy fibbed. ''By the way, The Prickly Pear is featuring a baked potato extravaganza tonight and they're promising 'a cornucopia of toppings.' Want to go?''

''Sure…no, wait.'' Chance took a slice out of the toaster. ''I've got to review some papers for a case tomorrow. It's a complicated custody battle.''

''What makes it complicated, or is that attorney-client privilege?''

''I can't discuss any details,'' he said. ''I can say that in my opinion the husband, who's a prominent individual, has done his best to make his wife look irresponsible so he can gain custody of their two children. Unfortunately, she's so naive he might get away with it.''

''You think she's the better parent?'' Although her sympathies instinctively went to the woman, Daisy wanted to be fair.

''She's the only real parent,'' Chance said. ''This guy doesn't even know who his kids' friends are or what they like to eat. He jeers when his son fumbles the ball in Little League and once scolded his daughter to tears because she got out of synch with the other girls during a dance recital. She was five years old.''

"Go prepare that case!" Daisy said. "You've got to win tomorrow."

"Church first." After finishing a second slice of toast, Chase cleared away his crumbs and returned the book to the counter.

Half an hour later, dressed and toting his overnight bag, he gave Daisy a kiss on the cheek. She moved away before the kiss could travel to her mouth.

The attraction between them grew stronger every day. To make matters worse, pregnancy, far from diminishing her desires, only increased them. She had to keep her wits about her.

"I'll see you Tuesday, if not before," Chance said.

"Good luck in court." The words sounded too impersonal, but Daisy didn't know what else to say.

The truth was, she would miss him. She missed him the moment he closed the door.

Later that morning, Daisy's mother dropped by with some newly finished maternity clothes. There was a pantsuit with a zipper top for easy breastfeeding, a swimsuit and a caftan suitable for gallery openings.

"You can wear it after you have the baby, too," Jeanine said as her daughter pirouetted in front of her. "There's a sash to use after you get your waistline back."

"They're wonderful, Mom. Thanks." Daisy hugged her.

"I'm sorry I missed seeing Chance." Jeanine had met him previously and liked him. "He's not getting restless?"

"Just the opposite," she said. "He keeps reminding me that he wants to marry me. In a light-hearted way, but underneath, he's serious."

"You're sure you aren't in love with him?"

Daisy wanted to reply that no, of course she wasn't in love. But her mother deserved the truth.

"I'm afraid I might be," she admitted. "It's wonderful, having him around. He's funny and considerate and he discusses our relationship as if we could work out our differences instead of fighting over them."

"Does he love you?"

"I don't know." As Daisy paced, the caftan swirled around her. "He likes me, I know that. And I like him. I've never dated a man who was a friend before."

"That's high praise. The men I've known were sometimes exciting, but no substitute for my friends," Jeanine said. "I hope things work out, for your sake. And for—have you picked a name for the baby yet?"

"Only Tom and Kitty, and I think we'll reserve those for our cats, if we ever get any." She smiled at the memory of their joking last night.

"I've never seen you this happy to be around a man." Her mother spread her sewing catalogs on the coffee table. "Now come here and tell me which of these clothes I should make next."

AT THE PRICKLY PEAR Bill and Frannie sat side by side at their table sampling each other's heaped-high potatoes. Several families from Mesa Blue had also chosen to enjoy the potato extravaganza, and Jeff Hawkin was tending bar.

Elise, Phoebe and Daisy lined up to top their potatoes. Having the three of them together was like old times, Daisy reflected, times that were passing much too quickly.

In her determination not to grow an inch before the wedding, Elise piled her potato with healthy chives, sprouts, nonfat grated cheese and plain yogurt. Phoebe, who had vowed to experiment, went for smoked salmon, seaweed, marinated tofu and capers.

Daisy didn't want to balloon during her pregnancy, but she could afford to indulge a little. So she chose bacon bits, low-fat cheese and nonfat sour cream.

"We need to talk about the reception," Elise said as they sat down.

"Is there a problem with the hotel?" Phoebe asked worriedly. She had reserved the ballroom at the same hotel for her own reception.

"Oh, no!" Elise said. "It's the music."

"I thought you hired a band," Daisy said.

"I did! But I need to pick some songs. Especially one for the first dance," Elise said. "I don't want to leave these things to the bandleader. He might start out with 'Having My Baby' and everybody'll think I'm pregnant."

"Not that there's anything wrong with pregnant brides," Phoebe said meaningfully.

"Or pregnant anythings," Elise amended. "I mean…oh, you know what I mean!"

"I didn't take it as criticism," Daisy returned mildly. "Besides, it's not a situation I would have chosen."

During her desperate-for-a-husband days, she'd considered the possibility of artificial insemination, but she believed a child deserved a two-parent home.

She hadn't counted on an accident. Even so, a child needed a father. Daisy didn't want to deny Tom or Kitty—she couldn't help thinking of the unborn baby by those affectionate nicknames—the best possible start in life.

Was she really considering Chance's proposal? Maybe so. Not just for the baby's sake, though. Only if he meant it from his heart.

Perhaps he did. Otherwise, why did he keep repeating it?

Elise and Phoebe went on talking. The song "We've Only Just Begun" was mentioned along with other romantic standards.

"I know which song they should play at my wedding," Daisy said dreamily. "'Some Enchanted Evening.' After all, that's how we met." Realizing what she'd just said, she added, "I mean, if Chance and I ever get married, which isn't likely."

Phoebe and Elise exchanged glances, but neither responded directly. Instead, Phoebe said, "Maybe I'll let Wyatt pick our music. He's a producer, so he's used to running the show."

They debated the merits of letting men having anything to do with weddings other than showing up. They finally agreed it would be gracious to at least give the appearance of being democratic.

"Most men don't want to do much, anyway," Elise said. "I asked James what kind of food he wanted for the dinner and he turned pale. Honestly! You'd think I'd asked him to cook it himself."

"The only thing I regret about my wedding is that I'm not ethnic," Phoebe said. "I know that sounds silly, but I've been to weddings where they celebrate colorful traditions or dance to special folk songs and it brings everyone together."

"I don't have to worry about bringing people together at my wedding," Elise said. "With six sisters and a brother, six brothers-in-law and my parents and aunts and uncles, most of the guests will be related."

"It's nice to have the whole family involved," Phoebe agreed.

"I wonder if my mother would make my gown,"

Daisy mused. "She'd do a fabulous job with white-on-white textures."

"It sounds like I may have a new sister-in-law," Elise said happily. "As a matter of fact, you'd be my first sister-in-law, since I've only got one brother."

"I guess I'd have to let you be a bridesmaid whether I wanted to or not," Daisy teased. "Oh, dear. Your six sisters wouldn't all expect to be included, would they?"

"I'm not having them in my wedding," her friend said. "So I can't see why they should expect to be in Chance's."

"Aren't they upset?" Phoebe asked.

"They're relieved," Elise told her. "They've gone through their own weddings and each other's weddings and they're sick of buying bridesmaid's dresses that hang in the closet afterward."

"You'll be happy to know that I like our dresses so much, I want Daisy to wear hers again at my wedding if she can still fit into it, and Elise, you can borrow mine," Phoebe said.

Daisy tried to imagine how she would look at six and a half months. "I might have to let out my dress. My mom could devise some side inserts."

"Just as long as they aren't black," Elise said. "Especially not for my wedding. I'm not allowing any black clothing except tuxedos."

"What if one of the guests wears black?" Phoebe asked.

"I'll throw a cloak over her!" They all laughed.

Chance would look striking in a tuxedo, Daisy thought as she finished her potato. He probably already owned one, since, according to his sister, he attended a lot of special events.

She didn't want to keep thinking about marrying the man. Yet she couldn't help visualizing him standing at the altar, a smile tugging his mouth as he watched her approach on her mother's arm.

Everyone else would fade from view, so that she saw only him, welcoming and warm. The playboy in love. The wanderer tamed.

The handsomest man she'd ever met, and the best male friend she'd ever had, would be waiting to take her hand and promise to love her always...

"Those bacon bits must be drugged," Phoebe said. "You've got the goofiest look on your face."

"She isn't goofy!" Elise protested. "The girl's in love."

"I am not!"

With one impulse both of her friends dug in their purses and produced mirrored compacts. When they held them up, Daisy saw herself reflected. Eyes bright. Cheeks pink. Lips parted.

"I have this thing for baked potatoes," she said.

Two compacts clicked shut in unison. "Yeah, right," said Phoebe.

Daisy focused on the conversation for the rest of the meal. It was embarrassing to be caught fantasizing, especially when both her friends knew who she was fantasizing about.

Besides, she wasn't in love. She cared a great deal about Chance. Sex with him that first night had been a revelation, but she'd been able to resist repeating the experience, hadn't she?

She was, at most, halfway to being in love, Daisy decided. That wasn't too far for her to retreat, if she chose to.

ON MONDAY MORNING she headed for the gallery, even though it was closed. Since she'd sold her first Personality Pot, her mind had been dancing with ideas for new ones, and she couldn't wait to get to work on them.

If more of her pots sold, she might seriously consider putting on her own show. There were a few openings in her schedule next spring. Did she dare reserve one for herself?

Chance believed she should. He wasn't the type of man to flatter anyone, Daisy was convinced. He wouldn't have expressed admiration for her work if he didn't mean it.

It had never occurred to her that being involved with a man meant having someone to encourage her. Someone on her side.

The rush-hour traffic moved sluggishly through the downtown. Stuck at a light, Daisy spotted a maroon luxury sedan ahead of her in the next lane.

It looked like Chance's new car, with the dealer plate still on. Had she been thinking of him so much that she was imagining things?

The light turned green. Her lane moved forward faster, and she glanced over.

It was unmistakably Chance at the wheel. He wasn't alone.

Beside him sat the overblown blonde he'd hugged outside a restaurant two months ago. The woman turned toward him and patted his arm, her face shining blissfully.

Daisy's heart nearly stopped beating.

She couldn't lie to herself. At this hour of the morning the logical explanation was that the pair had spent the night together and he was driving his lover to work.

She didn't want to believe it. The pain was too great, the betrayal too overwhelming.

It was true that she'd refused to sleep with him. In her observation, men wanted sex, and if they didn't get it from one woman, they went to another.

Not Chance. He couldn't be like that. Or had she been right all along to consider him a heartless playboy?

In a state of confusion, Daisy reached the gallery and parked. She sat in the car and tried to make sense of what she'd seen.

She couldn't. She could only ache with a huge upwelling sadness.

Last night she'd told herself that she wasn't in love. Well, she'd lied.

Chance's mellowness, his humor, his caring, infused every aspect of her world. He was the only man she'd ever pictured herself marrying. He was her happily ever after, her best friend and her baby's father.

He'd turned down an invitation to spend the evening with her, engaging her sympathy by claiming to be working on a custody case. Instead, he'd gone to another woman.

She hugged herself, fighting tears. They came, anyway, burning her eyes and trickling hotly down her cheeks.

Daisy recognized the tortured, helpless sensation twisting through her. It was how she'd felt when her father broke his promise about Christmas, when he failed to come on her birthday. Only much, much worse.

She felt stupid for believing in Chance. Angry at him for doing this to her. And utterly lost, because, in spite of everything, she loved him.

She couldn't give up this easily. She had to confront him and hope he could explain himself.

If he couldn't, she didn't know what she was going to do.

Chapter Twelve

Scarcely noticing what she was doing, Daisy changed into work clothes in her studio and began wedging clay. Her nerves felt as if they might explode. She couldn't possibly wait until tomorrow night to talk to Chance.

But she couldn't barge into his office, either. Besides, he'd said he would be in court. Had he told the truth? After what she'd seen this morning, she wasn't sure whether to believe him about anything.

Unexpectedly a ray of hope warmed her. Maybe the blonde was one of his sisters!

Hope died as quickly as it had sprung up. That doting expression on the woman's face hadn't looked sisterly. Besides, the woman bore no resemblance to Chance or Elise.

As she worked on the wheel, Daisy kept torturing herself with images of Chance and the blond woman. And with excuses for him. She might be a neighbor. A client. Or a paralegal who worked with him.

In her heart Daisy knew none of those explanations was right. She couldn't let her own longings blind her to painful reality.

By noon she couldn't stand the suspense any longer.

After straightening her studio, she cleaned up in the bathroom.

Face and hands scrubbed, Daisy yanked a brush through her hair, which was fuller than usual. One of the small benefits of pregnancy, she supposed.

She didn't look her best today, though. Hardly any makeup, and the casual dress emphasized her roundness.

What a cliché! She wrinkled her nose at her reflection in the mirror. The wronged, pregnant woman stalks into the man's office to confront her glamorous supplanter.

She didn't expect to see the blond woman, of course. Only Chance.

Daisy's chest tightened. Chance. She loved his smile. The way he filled a room with his vitality. The masculine smell of him.

She didn't think she could bear to learn that he didn't belong to her. But she had to face the truth.

She was as ready as she'd ever be. After looping her purse over one shoulder, Daisy locked the gallery and set out for his office.

IT HADN'T BEEN EASY, finding a chilled bottle of champagne near his office, but the occasion warranted it. Humming to himself, Chance strode along the sidewalk, hurrying before the August heat could penetrate the bottle under his arm.

He reached his office building's entrance right behind an auburn-haired woman who, from this angle, bore a startling resemblance to Daisy. When they reached the elevators and she turned, Chance saw that it *was* Daisy.

"Hey!" he said.

Her green eyes widened in surprise. "Oh!"

He hefted the paper sack holding the champagne. "You've got great timing. We're celebrating."

"Celebrating what?" she asked.

"I'll tell you upstairs." He presumed she'd come to ask him to lunch. She'd been loosening up recently, a development that he welcomed.

At his floor he guided her down the hall. It was her first visit to his office, an important occasion. "Right here."

She read the sign aloud. "Charles Foster, Attorney at Law." Beneath it, in smaller letters, "Divorce, Custody, Child Support, Adoptions. How ironic."

"Why is that?" He paused, not wanting to open the door until she explained.

"I was considering an adoption at first, for the baby's sake, remember? Of course, if I had, I wouldn't have come to you for my legal services." She didn't meet his eyes. Now that he paid closer attention, Daisy seemed tense.

"Is anything wrong?" Chance asked.

"We need to talk."

What could have happened since yesterday? "Sure. I hope you're not in a hurry, though."

"Well…"

He opened the door. Inside, two beaming faces greeted his arrival. Nell Beecham had set out paper plates on a table in the waiting room. Lanie Atherton, the client whose custody case he'd won this morning, was opening cartons of take-out Chinese food for their lunch.

"I found a bottle." Chance hoisted his package. "And look who else I found."

"Good!" Nell came to greet Daisy. "I'm sorry we

didn't get more chance to talk on Saturday night, but when I'm on a cat mission, I'm not at my most sociable.''

"This must be your fiancée!" Lanie hadn't grasped the fine distinction between a pregnant girlfriend and a betrothed, but then, Chance hoped there wasn't going to be a difference much longer. "I've been hoping to meet you. You're so lucky! This man is wonderful!"

She flung her arms around Daisy and gave her a smeary kiss on the cheek. That was Lanie's way of relating to people. With her mass of blond hair and overdone makeup, she gave the impression of being a sexpot, when in fact she was more of an eager-to-please puppy.

"Thanks." Daisy waited until Lanie was looking in another direction before wiping the lipstick off her cheek.

"You should have seen Chance in court today!" Lanie went on as she fussed with the Chinese food. "I can't believe we won! My ex-husband is such a snake. From what he said, you'd have thought I was the most irresponsible mother who ever lived, but by the time Chance got done, I received primary custody. My ex gets visitation, of course, but the kids live with me!"

"That's wonderful." Daisy's tone warmed.

"Let's not keep you standing. I remember when I was pregnant, my ankles used to swell." Nell ushered her to a couch by the table. "You make yourself comfortable."

"Thanks." As Daisy sat down, Chance spotted a trace of clay clinging to her temple.

"You've been working hard." Lowering himself beside her, he crumbled the clay between his fingers.

"Just throwing a few pots."

Lanie paused with a container of rice in one hand. "At who?"

"I meant, on the potter's wheel," Daisy said.

Lanie laughed. "How silly of me! Chance told me about those wonderful sculptures you make. I'm going to bring some of my friends by your gallery to take a look."

"I don't know if I'd call them sculptures. They're Personality Pots."

"Well, I want to see them. But not till I get my tires fixed." Lanie passed the food around. She'd insisted on providing it herself, despite Chance's offer to treat. "My husband slashed them this morning. At least, I figure it must have been him."

"That's awful," Daisy said.

"I didn't know how I was going to get to court, so I paged Chance, and he came right over. I just love his new car! There'll be lots of room for your baby and the other kids when you have them."

Daisy was smiling broadly. "Could I have some of that shrimp? It smells wonderful."

She didn't drink any champagne, enjoying a ginger ale instead. Other than that, she joined right in the conversation. Chance was delighted that she'd come. He wanted to share every special occasion with her.

As they were cleaning up, he remembered that she'd mentioned wanting to talk to him. "You came to see me about something?" he prompted.

"Oh, that." Daisy shrugged. "I wondered...I mean...would you like to join me for dinner tonight?"

"Sure," he said. "What can I bring?"

"Just yourself." She collected her purse. "Around six?"

"Great." He didn't think that's what she'd meant to discuss, but he couldn't dwell on the subject now.

He had an appointment with Abner Ewing, who was coming to sign his separation papers. Chance intended to try one more time to persuade the man to seek counseling.

A few minutes later Abner arrived punctually, and Nell showed him to the inner office. The repair shop owner had lost weight since July and seemed more relaxed, Chance noted.

"You look good," he said.

"I feel better." The man cleared his throat. "I won't be signing those papers after all."

"Care to tell me why?"

"It was miserable being by myself," Abner said. "I told Janet I wanted custody, that it wasn't enough to see the kids every other weekend. You know what she said?"

"Please tell me." Chance leaned forward.

"She said that every other weekend would be more often than I see them now." Abner gave an embarrassed shake of the head. "She was right. Even when I'm home, I'm watching a game on TV. If I did get custody, I wouldn't know what to do with the kids."

"You came in to sign separation papers, not sue for custody," Chance reminded him.

"Yeah, well, Janet moved back in and we made a deal," the man said. "I come home for dinner at least four nights a week, and I take the kids out on Saturday afternoons, just the three of us. On Sunday night, her mother baby-sits and she and I go out to dinner."

"How's it working?"

"I found out I didn't know my kids or my wife, either," Abner said ruefully. "It's a whole new experience. I can't swear I won't slip into my old habits, but I'm willing to try to keep our marriage together.''

"Congratulations." Getting to his feet, Chance shook hands. "I'm glad you won't be needing my services.''

"I don't much like lawyers, but you're all right." The man went out the door whistling.

Chance wished every day could be as upbeat as this one. And he still had dinner with Daisy to look forward to.

As she prepared zucchini lasagne, Daisy tried to figure out why she felt exhilarated and a little scared at the same time.

The exhilaration wasn't hard to explain. The discovery of Chance's innocence relieved and thrilled her.

The scary part, she supposed, was admitting, even to herself, that she loved him. She was on the brink of taking a huge step into the unknown, of trusting Chance with her happiness.

Not that she needed to make such a huge decision right away. Or even to tell him how she felt.

But she'd never come this close before in her own heart to making a commitment. True, Daisy had been seeking a husband for the past year, hoping to find the right man to cherish her and their child. When she'd pictured him, though, she'd imagined someone…safe.

Chance would never be safe. If she wasn't careful, he would roll over her like a bulldozer. How could she be sure of maintaining control of her life?

When the doorbell rang, Daisy wasn't ready to see him. She fluttered around the kitchen for a few seconds, trying to compose herself, before giving up and going to let him in.

Her nerves steadied when she saw him. There was a calmness and a good cheer about Chance that soothed her.

He presented her with a box of chocolates. "Since it isn't our usual night, I feel like we're stealing this time together. Which makes it even more fun."

She opened the box and inhaled the scent. "Nut filled, my favorites."

"I guessed," he said. "Actually, Nell guessed. She's my secret weapon. She likes you, you know." After closing the door, he strolled across the living room and into the kitchen. "What culinary masterpiece are you concocting?"

Daisy scurried behind him with the box of chocolates. "Let's skip dinner and eat dessert."

"That isn't healthy," he said in mock reproof.

"Tom or Kitty won't mind." While pretending to protest, Daisy set the box aside for later. "Besides, did you know chocolate contains antioxidants? It keeps you young."

"It also contains caffeine, which isn't good for the baby, but I won't tell anyone if you won't," Chance said. "Now what did you really want to talk to me about this afternoon?"

The suddenness of the question stopped Daisy cold. "That's not fair!"

"What isn't?"

"You caught me off guard."

"It's a lawyer trick," he said. "Makes for a productive cross-examination."

"Does it? Oh, I think the lasagne's done." She grabbed her pot holders and opened the oven.

"You're changing the subject."

"That's an antilawyer trick." Mozzarella cheese

bubbled on top, slightly browned. She removed the baking dish carefully. "Perfect. It needs to cool for about fifteen minutes, which gives me time to bake the bread."

"You bake bread?" he said.

"No, I just toast it." Daisy picked up a cookie sheet covered with slices of French bread, to which she'd added margarine and garlic salt.

"Close enough."

She slipped the bread into the oven, set the timer for a few minutes and turned to face Chance. His tie, she noticed, was crooked, as if inviting her to straighten it. "Did Nell rough you up so you'd look touchable?"

She'd meant it as a joke and was surprised to see a glint of embarrassment in his eyes. "She did make a few alterations to my appearance as I was leaving."

"She had a good eye." Daisy caught his tie but, instead of straightening it, she gripped the knot. "This is kind of like a leash, isn't it?"

"You planning to take me for a walk?" Chance cocked one eyebrow suggestively. He had only to take a step forward, and she'd be backed against the table. Fair game. And, in her present mood, unable to resist.

"No." She let go. "The bread. It only takes a few minutes."

"To heck with the bread."

"Don't swear in front of the baby."

"I said 'heck.' Do you know how difficult that is for a grown man?"

"Grown men need to practice restraint," Daisy said.

He advanced, trapping her between his hard body and the table. "I'm tired of practicing restraint. How about a little unrestrained—" The timer sounded. He flinched but didn't stir. "Ignore it."

"Burned bread will smell up the whole condo," Daisy said.

Chance glowered. Finally he backed off enough for her to slip away.

Daisy set the cookie sheet on the unlit stovetop to cool. She'd made the salad earlier. Now all they had to do was wait a short time and dinner would be ready. But she wasn't hungry or, at least, she wasn't hungry for food.

"Come here." Catching her hand, Chance led her into the living room, dropped into an armchair and pulled her onto his lap. "Now you're going to tell me whatever it was that you wanted to talk to me about at lunch."

There was no distance left between them, emotionally or physically. Daisy was intimately aware of his muscular thighs beneath her derriere and the intent way he watched her. Waiting.

"I saw you driving to work with Lanie," she said. "I'd seen you both together in front of a restaurant a couple of months ago. I thought you...the two of you..."

His forehead furrowed. "That I was sleeping with her?"

"It was the obvious explanation," Daisy said sheepishly. "That's why I came to your office. To ask you about her."

"I'm glad you did, but..." He framed her face with his palms, his gaze holding hers. "How could you believe I would sleep with another woman after I'd proposed to you? When you're having my baby and we're practically living together?"

She felt guilty and unreasonable and afraid she'd offended him. "Elise used to tell us what a playboy you were. That you had a different woman for every occasion. When I met you, you didn't seem that way, but I don't trust my own judgment when it comes to men, and especially you.''

Understanding dawned in his eyes, which were, she observed at close range, not merely gray but subtly iridescent with hints of violet. ''Is that why you ran away the first night, after you found out who I was?''

She nodded, unable to speak through the lump in her throat.

''Oh, Daisy.'' Chance wrapped his arms around her and pulled her against his chest. She nestled into him, the day's uncertainty evaporating. ''I'm not anything like that. I never settled down because I never found the right woman.''

''You did once,'' she reminded him.

''I thought I did,'' he corrected. ''My relationship with Gillian was tied up with our ambitions and dreams. If she'd really been the right woman, we would have stayed together.''

''You still have ambitions and dreams,'' Daisy pointed out.

''Are you looking for an excuse to push me away?''

''No.''

He stroked her hair. ''Sure, there's a part of me that quickens at the thought of making my mark in the world. Of handling major cases, getting that adrenaline rush, seeing my name in the headlines. But that has nothing to do with Gillian. Or with anything. I'm a grown man, Daisy, and I'm not stupid enough to turn away from happiness when I'm holding it in my arms.''

''Are you angry?'' she asked. ''Because I was so foolish?''

''You weren't foolish,'' Chance said. ''You were

protecting yourself. Daisy, it took courage for you to come to my office today. And I'm grateful that you told me the truth tonight.''

"Is this what you mean by communicating?'' she asked.

He nodded. "But you know what? The best kind of communication is nonverbal. Allow me to make a small demonstration.''

As he brought her mouth down to his, it occurred to Daisy that their food was going to get cold. And that she didn't care.

CHANCE ONLY MEANT to kiss her. He was pleasantly relaxed after a long day, and it seemed the height of luxury simply to hold Daisy and stroke her soft hair.

His body had other ideas, he discovered. The pressure of her breasts against his chest stirred tongues of flame inside, and he ached to feel the silkiness of her skin directly against his.

Her top had a front zipper that slid down easily in his grasp. Against his shoulder, Daisy moaned.

Her response further excited Chance. He eased the top open and traced the lacy rim of her bra with his thumb. Her breasts felt full and, through the fabric, he could see the nipples harden.

"Mine,'' he whispered, and, angling her to suit his pleasure, ran his tongue along the path his thumb had blazed. She gasped and cupped his day-roughened cheek in her hand.

Maneuvering her easily, Chance removed the bra and let his breath warm her swelling breasts. Her body shifted against his, responding rhythmically.

He gathered Daisy in his arms and lifted her from the armchair. With long strides, he carried her into the bedroom, his blood heating with anticipation.

Chapter Thirteen

After tonight Daisy knew she would never be the same. Sleeping with Chance once had changed her forever, but she hadn't known that at the time. Sleeping with him again was a deliberate leap into the future.

And a sheer, unadulterated joy.

For once, she let him take charge of her. It was what he wanted, and what she wanted, too. Because at last she trusted him.

Pregnancy made her acutely sensitive to the touch, unable to bear anything tentative. His decisiveness was exactly what she needed.

She loved the smoothness of Chance's shirt against her skin as she unworked the buttons. And the roughness of his chest, tantalizing her breasts.

When he stripped off her pants, she welcomed the rush of cool air and the heat of his body, replacing it.

She was ready for him almost immediately, and he sensed it. What a fierce man he was, and yet how gentle, as he lifted himself over her and united them with a long, easy thrust.

Daisy cried out happily and played her hands along the contoured muscles of his arms. Chance was like a sculpture, tactilely fascinating, aesthetically pleasing. But so much more.

His eyes shone as his mouth brushed hers, a reminder that this went beyond a mere physical joining. They were uniting their souls as well as their bodies.

Daisy melted into him as his movements grew stronger and faster. Conscious thought vanished.

They moved as one being, faster and faster, accelerating to the rim of sensation. And floated over it, landing in a buoyant warm sea.

Daisy held Chance tight. She couldn't consider what the consequences of tonight might be or where their emotions would take them. It was too new, this sense of surrender and of triumph.

It was enough, right now, simply to enjoy being with him.

LATER, AFTER EATING DINNER and making love to Daisy again, Chance lay beside her with an unaccustomed sense of contentment. Everything was falling into place.

They hadn't discussed their long-term plans. He doubted she'd appreciate it if he rushed her, but he didn't intend to wait too long.

His sister's wedding was less than three weeks away. By then Chance expected that he and Daisy would be ready to announce their engagement. She could sell her condo and move into his house before Christmas.

It had taken a long time for the barriers to fall, he thought lazily as he played with a lock of her auburn hair. Already half-asleep, she wiggled closer, endearingly warm.

Reconciling their differences, however, had been easier than Chance dared hope. Once Daisy overcame her fear of sharing her feelings, they'd found each other again.

From now on communication should get easier and easier. With a satisfied yawn, he curled around her protectively.

DAISY WAS STILL FLOATING on a cloud on Friday of the following week, when her second Personality Pot sold. What pleased her was not just the sale itself but the person who bought it.

Arturo Alonzo ran the Nouveau Ceramics gallery in Scottsdale and served as president of the Arizona Craft Arts Association. Although Daisy had met him several times, he'd never taken much notice of her until now.

Not only did he decide to buy the vase, he requested a private viewing of the more than a dozen pots stored in her workshop. He spent considerable time studying them and asking questions about her glazes and techniques.

"A friend told me recently that you had done some exceptional work. That's why I came in," he told Daisy as he accompanied her to the front of the gallery to complete his purchase. "How long have you been making these?"

"Just a short time. It's a new idea I'm exploring." With sudden resolve, she decided to stop downplaying herself. It wouldn't hurt to let Arturo know that she took pride in her work. "As a matter of fact, I'm scheduling my own one-woman show for next spring."

"Good," Arturo said. "I hope it's in May."

Pieces chinged into place, slot machine-like, in Daisy's brain. Although Scottsdale's main art event was its annual Celebration of Fine Arts, held from late January to late March, next year the Craft Arts Association was working with an international ceramics group to stage a symposium that would draw artists from around the world.

At Arizona State University, the guest artists would give lectures and demonstrations. They, along with symposium officials and reporters from ceramics publications around the world, would also tour selected galleries in the Phoenix-Scottsdale area.

Considerable distinction would fall on the Arizona craftsmen and women whose exhibits were included on the tour. And it would take place in May.

Arturo seemed to be suggesting that Daisy's show might qualify. That fact wasn't lost on Sean, whose freckled face lit with excitement as he hovered in the background.

Mentally Daisy reviewed her gallery's schedule of exhibitions for next spring. The calendar wasn't filled yet. "Yes, it will be in May."

"I'd like to propose your exhibit for the international tour," Arturo said. "You wouldn't mind if some members of our executive committee drop by to check out your work?"

"I'd be delighted," Daisy said. "Would you like me to send you some photographs?" Sean, an excellent photographer, could take them and get them printed right away.

"That would be terrific."

She managed to contain her excitement until Arturo had departed. As soon as he was out of earshot, she and Sean whooped and danced around the gallery.

"I can't believe it!" Daisy said. "Chance told me I should give myself a show, but I thought he was being kind."

"Next year is going to be *your* year!" her assistant

announced. "You'll become a mom in January and an international superstar in May."

"Well, not quite!" Even the best-known ceramists came nowhere near the fame of rock stars or clothing designers. "But it will boost my reputation, and the gallery's, too."

"You're on your way!" cheered Sean.

Daisy laughed. "Wait till I tell Chance!"

"So when's the wedding?" asked Sean.

"A week from Saturday."

He gaped. "Excuse me?"

"Elise's wedding. It's a week from Saturday," Daisy repeated.

"I meant *your* wedding."

"Oh!" She blushed. "I don't know. I mean, we haven't formalized anything."

Several times this past week Chance's comments had made it clear he took it for granted that she would accept his proposal. And she intended to.

The only point troubling Daisy was the way he kept making assumptions. That she would marry him and live in his house, for instance.

But he wasn't expecting anything unreasonable. There was nothing she disagreed with.

With luck, there never would be.

"I can hardly wait to tell him about Arturo." Chance still stayed over three nights a week, but tonight, Friday, wasn't one of them. "Maybe I'll go by his office at lunchtime and see if he's in."

"That would be now," Sean pointed out.

"You can eat first," she said politely.

"I'm brown bagging," he said. "Go."

Daisy didn't argue. She couldn't wait to share her news with Chance.

"YOU HAVE TO HEAR ME OUT." Gillian's voice came over the phone strong and confident. "I'll be in Phoenix next Thursday and Friday. We'll start with lunch Thursday at—what's that little place near you?—Le Bistro Français."

"You're not coming out just to see me, are you?" Chance said.

"I've got some other business," she told him. "But you're the main attraction."

"All right," he said. "Shall I pick you up at the airport?"

"I'll rent a car." She prized her independence, he supposed. "Make a reservation for noon."

"I'll look forward to it."

Chance didn't flatter himself that her interest was personal, nor did he want it to be. The few times he'd spoken to Gillian during the past few years, he'd found her more and more obsessed with her career. Like now.

The law firm of Roker, Sandringham, Wiley and Farrar had decided to expand into family law for the benefit of its business and political clients. They would be able to have their marital and custody matters handled discreetly without engaging another law firm.

Gillian had recommended Chance for the new division. After reviewing his records, the partners had agreed that he fit their firm's professional image.

Chance guessed that they liked the way he'd kept a low profile. While they could probably secure a better-known divorce attorney, the firm's clients might not want to work with someone known for handling scandalous cases.

Gillian hadn't given any details, or said how many attorneys would be joining the new operation. All that could wait until her arrival next Thursday.

It would be a coup for Gillian to bring one of her friends into the law firm, particularly if Chance proceeded to distinguish himself. And she would have an ally in what he didn't doubt was an ongoing battle for position and advancement within Roker, Sandringham, Wiley and Farrar.

As for him, he hadn't sought a change in his career. But it would be crazy to pass up the opportunity without giving it full consideration.

Chance didn't like the prospect of moving away from his large family. And he doubted Daisy would be happy about moving so far from her mother and friends, especially when she was having a baby.

But a long-suppressed eagerness welled inside him. Washington, D.C. The thought of living and working in the nation's capital sent his adrenaline surging.

For the past ten years Chance had suppressed his yearning to be a player in major events. He'd almost forgotten how much he wanted to achieve big things and face new challenges.

He was thirty-five years old. This might be his last opportunity to make his old dream come true.

DAISY DIDN'T BELIEVE what she was hearing. Or, rather, she didn't want to believe it.

Sitting across his desk from her, Chance glowed with excitement. He was so thrilled about his news that he didn't seem to notice her stunned reaction.

He might be moving to Washington, D.C., taking on a high-pressure job, working eighty hours a week. Even as he acknowledged that such a change would be difficult for Daisy, he took it for granted that she would go with him.

During the past few months, Chance had raised the

issue of communication several times. Yet today she felt as if they'd never communicated clearly about anything. He didn't seem to understand her at all.

The timing couldn't have been worse. Daisy had finally begun to achieve some recognition as an artist, yet a child's future happiness hung in the balance. Did she really have to choose between her career and this marriage?

She couldn't flat-out say, *No, I won't go*. Of all the relationships in her life, this was the last one she wanted to end in a quarrel.

It was safer to try to arouse his own doubts. "Is this really what you want?" she asked. "I thought you enjoyed helping your clients."

"I do. But Arizonians aren't the only ones who have family problems." Chance gave her a crooked grin.

"I'm sure it's very flattering…"

He leaned forward and spoke earnestly. "One of my law professors told me that if I weren't so distracted by having to work my way through school I could have been one of his top students. It troubles me that I may be wasting my talents here."

"You've done a lot of good," she said.

He ran one hand through his hair, disarranging its trim perfection. "Our gifts are precious. I believe we owe them a chance to flourish, just as we owe the same opportunity to our children."

"Speaking of children, when would you see ours?" Daisy asked. "You'd be working all the time."

He frowned. "There's such a thing as quality time. Although Gillian doesn't have kids, maybe she can offer some insight into how other families manage."

This wasn't working. Daisy had to risk a stronger stance. "I don't like this idea, Chance. My gallery…"

He came around the desk and, sliding into the chair beside hers, cupped her small hands in his large ones. "There's no reason you can't open a gallery in D.C. I'll stake you to the initial expenses. Heck, you could make quite a splash. This might be a great opportunity for you."

How could he expect her to find the time and energy to start over with a new baby and an absentee husband? "It's not that simple!"

"Please support me in this." His gray eyes burned into hers. "If I don't give my dream one more shot, it will haunt me forever. Whatever the problems are, we'll solve them together. That is, if I decide to take the job, which is still a big *if.*"

"I want you to be happy. But I want to be happy, too," she said.

When she came here today, Daisy had meant to tell him about Arturo Alonzo. But she couldn't do it right now. This development in her career was too important to use as a mere bargaining chip.

"All I'm going to do is listen to what Gillian has to say." Playfully Chance traced her nose with his forefinger. "I couldn't wait to tell you about it. I hoped you'd be pleased."

Pleased about being ripped from her friends and gallery? Pleased about being expected to go live in a strange place while her husband immersed himself in his cases?

Daisy bit her tongue. The arguments in her head sounded strident to her. She'd destroyed her last relationship with futile, angry words, and this one meant infinitely more to her.

"I guess I'll have to wait and see." Maybe he

wouldn't want the job, after all. "I'd better get back to work."

Chance escorted her through his office. At the reception desk, Nell Beecham sat scowling at some papers.

The secretary wasn't happy about this development, either, Daisy thought. But Chance, absorbed in his scenarios for the future, seemed oblivious.

DAYLIGHT AND HEAT lingered into Friday evening. Early September was like summer in Phoenix, and the three friends seized the opportunity to take a late swim.

Daisy's swimsuit stretched tautly across her enlarging shape as she dog paddled beside her friends. Inside, baby Kitty—or was it Tom—squirmed as if she too were trying to swim.

Soon Elise and Phoebe would be married and there would be no more casual get-togethers after work, Daisy thought. She was glad for them, but it tore at her heart that, after coming so close to finding the ideal man for herself, she might be on the brink of losing him.

Jeff Hawkin wandered by the pool, sweeping up leaves. "Aren't you bartending tonight?" Daisy asked.

"Not until later," he said. "Bill suggested I stick around. Frannie's baking a special dessert, he said."

She'd been hoping to have a private moment to talk with her friends. So she was grateful when one of Mesa Blue's younger, bikini-clad residents showed up to flirt with Jeff in a far corner of the pool area.

"Have you talked to your brother today?" she asked Elise.

"Uh-oh," her friend said. "If you're referring to Chance as 'your brother,' you must be mad at him."

"He wants to move to Washington, D.C." Daisy struggled to be fair. "I mean, he might. He's received a job offer."

She filled in her friends on the details. Gillian. Big-name clients. A large salary. Long hours.

"That's rotten," Elise said. "He can't drag you from pillar to post as if you were his pet poodle."

"On the other hand, ambition isn't something to take lightly," noted Phoebe, whose own ambition kept her nose to the grindstone earning a degree in biochemistry.

"I'm ambitious, too, and I got a big break of my own today." Daisy told them about Arturo Alonzo and the May gallery tour. "It would be a huge honor."

"Did you tell Chance?" Elise asked.

Daisy shook her head, sending drops of water flying. "He wasn't listening to anything I said. If he blew off something so important to me, I might have yelled at him and stalked out. I didn't want an ugly scene."

"I can't imagine you losing your temper. You're always so easygoing," Phoebe said.

"My brother can make anyone lose her temper," countered Elise. "When he gets into one of his arrogant moods, there's no reasoning with him."

"My last two boyfriends—well, my only two important boyfriends—both left after we argued," Daisy confessed. "It was partly my fault. I let my anger build up until I exploded."

"Surely you could talk to him calmly," Phoebe said.

"I tried, I really did," Daisy said. "How can I communicate with him if he dismisses everything I say? I'm just hoping he'll change his mind before we reach all-out nuclear war."

"Change his mind? You think he's already made it up?" said Elise.

"It sure sounds like it."

Two voices singing off-key in the dusk dragged her attention to the other end of the courtyard. Frannie and Bill, belting out a ragged version of the song "Together" from *Gypsy,* marched toward them carrying a cake on a large cookie sheet.

When they got closer, she saw that the cake was shaped like a cat, with striped icing. Small blue candles in the eyes glowed through the twilight.

"We're glad we caught you all together tonight," Bill said, including Jeff and his female friend in the group. "We're celebrating Frannie's and my engagement."

Smiling broadly, his red-haired companion extended her left hand. Among her many rings, a new gold one with diamond chips stood out.

"You're engaged? Congratulations!" Phoebe hopped out of the pool. "I'd hug you, but you'd get all wet."

"We have you four to thank," Frannie said. "If you hadn't done your best to bring us together, it might not have happened."

"I didn't do anything," Jeff protested modestly.

"Inviting us both to The Prickly Pear that night?" Bill said. "That was important!"

"Have you set a date?" Phoebe asked.

"We're going to Las Vegas at the end of the month," Frannie said. "I went through one big wedding with my first marriage. This time I just want to concentrate on my husband."

"Then we're going camping for our honeymoon,"

Bill said. "Of course, we don't want to stay away too long."

"We can't leave Nell and Sarita to take care of the feral cats by themselves," Frannie explained. "Besides, that tortoiseshell cat is getting friendlier all the time. We don't want to lose track of him."

"There's always room for one more cat." Bill didn't flinch. Apparently, he'd gained an appreciation for felines, or perhaps resolved himself to like them for the sake of his wife-to-be.

Happy as she was for them, Daisy couldn't restrain a pang of envy. Bill was willing to meet his fiancée halfway. There really were such men in the world. Why hadn't she found one?

But she didn't want anyone other than Chance. She treasured his dynamic personality and take-charge attitude, except when they ran roughshod over her needs.

For once in her life she'd allowed herself to love a man without restraint. If only she could keep him!

Daisy ached to be like Frannie, bouncing with joy, basking in the congratulations of friends as they admired her ring. Maybe she should consider operating her gallery until next summer, then relocating to Washington.

She could still be part of the May gallery tour. And she wouldn't have to lose Chance.

Besides, how could she deny her child the right to grow up with his or her father? Chance had promised to spend quality time together, and so far he'd always kept his promises.

The high-handed manner in which he'd treated her still rankled. But Daisy wasn't ready to give him up. She doubted she ever would be.

Chapter Fourteen

On Sunday after church Chance took his parents to see his house. They'd visited it before, of course, but not since he'd added the sculpture and paintings that made it a showplace.

Margaret Foster raved over each piece, claiming to see Daisy's personal touch in every item despite Chance's assurances that he'd made his own selections. Ever since they learned that he was seriously dating the woman they'd known for years as Elise's friend, his parents had gone out of their way to let him know they approved.

Sam spoke less, although he was obviously impressed. Chance especially valued his father's perceptions. He might never have made a lot of money in business, but that was because Sam had devoted so much time to his eight kids, to their school and to the community.

"I'm glad you like it," Chance said as they sipped coffee in the courtyard after their mini-tour.

"I'm curious about one thing," His father said. "What are you going to do with this artwork if you move to D.C.? The architecture is real different in that part of the country. These pieces might not look as good in your new home.''

''I haven't had time to think about it,'' Chance admitted. It had been only two days since Gillian called, and he'd had other things on his mind.

Last night he and Daisy had gone to The Prickly Pear with a group of friends to toast Frannie and Bill's engagement. Afterward, Daisy had suffered such bad heartburn—due to the pregnancy, she'd said—that she'd taken an antacid and curled up alone in bed.

She hadn't wanted to be touched, not even stroked a little. Chance missed the contact.

She hadn't wanted to discuss his job offer. Each time he'd tried to reassure her about it, she'd withdrawn even more. If she was angry with him, why didn't she say so?

He knew she would adjust and thrive in the new circumstances. Daisy was a smart, talented, energetic woman. Soon she would come to see that there could be advantages for both of them in moving to a larger, more sophisticated arena.

But right now she didn't seem happy about making such a major transition. The prospect of having to sell his house and dispose of the artwork, after the time and love he'd put into them, didn't thrill Chance, either.

''Maybe I'll rent it out,'' he said. ''We could lease a place in Virginia or Maryland for a while.''

''I won't like having my grandchild so far away,'' his mother said. ''I don't mean to be selfish. But it hasn't been the same with Anita's kids as with my other grandchildren, you know.''

His sister Anita, the third oldest girl, had moved to Ohio a few years ago with her husband and baby daughter. Since then, they'd had a son. They visited

Phoenix a couple of times each year, but the children were practically strangers.

"It won't be like that. We'll visit often." His words, even to him, rang hollow. "Okay, I agree, there's a downside to moving away. As I told you earlier, I haven't made up my mind."

"You then proceeded to enumerate all the advantages of going," Sam pointed out.

"You told us Daisy took it well," said his mother. "Didn't she raise any objections?"

"A few," Chance admitted. "Nothing insurmountable."

"Maybe you should consider getting some counseling before you decide."

His mother might have been parroting his own words, issued on many occasions to his siblings and clients. For some reason Chance found them irritating now.

"We have good communications skills," he said. "We can work this out for ourselves. In fact, we *are* working it out."

"I'm glad to hear it," his father said mildly. "Now, I wanted to ask your opinion about that computer you gave me for Christmas. It's a little slow downloading material from the Internet and I'm considering upgrading. What do you think?"

It was a pleasure, Chance found, to discuss something technical and neat and easy to quantify. If only life were like that.

ON THURSDAY MORNING the gallery had another distinguished visitor. Ione Marshall, an art professor from the university who had helped organize the symposium, came to see Daisy's work.

"Arturo raved about you." Small and slender, the sixtyish professor had a wing of silver hair. Her sharp eyes and quick manner testified to her energy and intelligence, but there was nothing overbearing about her. "I had to see for myself."

"I'm honored." Daisy escorted her into the studio. During the past few days, she'd rearranged the lighting and positioned the Personality Pots for better viewing.

The major distraction today was some noisy work on a city water main down the block. And the knowledge that at this very moment Chance was dining with Gillian at the French bistro, the first of several meetings planned for today and tomorrow.

Resolutely Daisy put those matters out of her head and focused on her visitor.

"These are clever." Ione smiled at a pot that sported an angelic boy's head, complete with encircling halo, above the muscular arms and shoulders of a bodybuilder. "I like your sense of humor."

"For my show, I plan to make some themed series." The concept had struck Daisy a few days earlier. "Perhaps a half dozen caricatures of U.S. presidents done in the manner of Greek statues, with laurel garlands and bare torsos."

"That's wonderful!" Ione nodded for emphasis. "You know, I've been contacted by some German artists who are organizing their own symposium. They asked me to recommend a ceramic sculptor from Arizona."

"There are so many fine ones!" Daisy blurted.

"Yes, but some of them are overcommitted, and one man won't travel by air," Ione said. "I don't mean to make this sound like a backhanded compliment..."

"I don't fool myself that I've suddenly become the most talented person around," Daisy said.

"Anyway, I'd like to send an outstanding representative," Ione said. "Arizona doesn't always get the respect it deserves. I'm glad to know we have one more topnotch ceramist."

"Thank you." Daisy couldn't bear to mention that she might not be living in Arizona much longer.

GILLIAN KEPT GLANCING around the restaurant as if looking for important people. It must have become a habit in Washington.

Sitting across from Chance, she looked terrific with her smooth blond hair styled in a pageboy and her figure fashionably lean in an elegant suit. The summer heat hadn't wilted her a bit, but then, he'd heard that Washington was not only hot in the summer but humid as well, so she must be used to it.

Her high cheekbones and slightly hooded eyes had taken on definition since their college days. There was something larger than life about her, he decided.

"You mentioned you're going to be a father but you didn't say anything about marriage," she observed. "This doesn't sound like the old-fashioned guy I used to know."

"Daisy's been reluctant to accept my proposal." He set his menu aside. Dining here so often, he knew what he wanted to eat. "She's coming around, though."

"She'd be willing to relocate?" Gillian asked.

"I think so. She owns a gallery down the street." Chance felt a twinge of guilt at his cavalier assumption that Daisy would be willing to start over for his sake. But she could reach an international clientele, something she wasn't likely to do here. "I'm sure she'd be even more successful in Washington."

"And she'll have motherhood to keep her busy." When the waiter approached, Gillian ordered the salade Niçoise with dressing on the side. Chance chose the salmon.

He wondered why he felt uncomfortable discussing Daisy with Gillian. It wasn't a matter of fearing his old girlfriend would feel displaced; he knew that much.

Maybe it was because he couldn't possibly convey what a unique and special woman he had found. It bothered him to hear her dismissed as if she were just another hausfrau, not that he supposed any woman really fit that stereotype.

"Let's talk about Roker, Sandringham, Wiley and Farrar." Gillian took a sip of ice water before continuing. "Salaries, benefits, advancement opportunities. I think you'll be pleased."

Chance was more interested in hearing about the clients he'd be working with and the firm's ethical policies. He wasn't running this meeting, though, so he sat back to listen.

AFTER IONE LEFT, Daisy and Sean took down an exhibit called "Paper on Paper." The array of fantastic wall hangings and floor-mounted works had been created largely of layered paper in dazzling colors.

They set these aside to make room for pieces unloaded this morning for an exhibit opening Sunday afternoon. Normally, it would have opened on Saturday night, but Daisy had cleared her schedule for Elise's 4:00 p.m. wedding.

Called "DinoCouture" and created by Tempe artist Elroy McGinnis, the sculptures were life-size models of bones wired together to form a variety of dinosaurs. The result would have been at home in a science museum except that the pseudoskeletons wore amusing bits of clothing: argyle socks on one, a baseball cap on another, a bowtie, a Batman cape and so on.

"You've really got the ball rolling now," said Sean, who'd been agog during Ione's visit. "Daisy, I hate to say this, but you can't move to Washington."

"I have to consider—" Feeling torn in two pieces, she stopped. She didn't want to discuss her personal situation in any detail with her assistant. Much as she liked Sean, the situation called for discretion. "I'll figure out something."

A metallic clanking in the wall made them both jump. "What was that?" he asked.

There'd been thumping noises earlier from water gushing sporadically through the aging pipes. "Whatever they're doing to that water main, I wish they'd finish."

"Whoa! What's that?' Sean indicated a bulge in the plaster.

"Oh, no!" Daisy stared in horror at a growing wet stain. "One of the pipes must have burst. We'll have water everywhere!"

The gallery was empty except for one of the DinoCoutures, which they grabbed and carted out. By the time the two of them returned, water was spurting through a newly formed hole in the wall.

"I'll call the city. And a plumber, too." Sean ran for the phone.

At the rate water was flowing, it wouldn't take long to spill beyond the single gallery. The adjacent space was filled with vulnerable paper pieces, most of them temporarily propped on the floor.

Insurance might cover most of the damage, but it couldn't replace the artwork. Frantically Daisy snatched up the nearest piece and hauled it into the back.

THE ATTORNEYS' SALARIES that Gillian cited were stratospheric. Not to mention large bonuses for winning lawsuits and settlements.

And Chance couldn't avoid a surge of excitement when she got around to listing some of the firm's best-known clients. Diplomats, politicians, chief executives, media giants.

"We don't expect family law to be as lucrative as some of our other areas," Gillian conceded. "However, it should be worth a lot in terms of client loyalty."

"What kind of hours are we talking about?" Chance asked. "Usually family law involves more regular hours than criminal or tort work."

"At Roker, Sandringham, Wiley and Farrar, we have to be available whenever and wherever we're needed." She spoke in staccato style, picking up steam. "If a client wants you to fly to Saudi Arabia for a consultation, you go."

Through the many-paned window, Chance saw a group of people gathering down the street. Some stood staring into a building, while others ran inside and carted out what appeared to be brightly colored sculptures.

With a jolt he realized there must be a serious problem at Native Art. A fire? A structural collapse?

"Gillian, I'm sorry to cut you off, but there appears to be an emergency at Daisy's gallery."

She followed his gaze. "Oh, dear." For a moment

he thought she might try to dissuade him from going, but then she shrugged. "We've accomplished enough for our first meeting."

They'd agreed to meet tonight and again tomorrow. To go over more specifics and, Chance assumed, for her to try to sign him up before she left Phoenix on Saturday morning. "I'll get the—"

"I'll take care of the bill." Gillian gave him a knowing smile. "You run and check on your friend. I'll be along in a minute."

"Great." It would be good for Daisy to meet Gillian. In the future they might be seeing a fair amount of each other.

CITY WORKERS HAD PROMISED to cut off the water, but the level inside the gallery was still rising. Soaked, her hair sticking to her face, Daisy pulled more of the pieces to safety.

Thank goodness for Sean and a few Good Samaritans! But if they didn't work faster, the dozen remaining paper artworks were going to get soaked.

She didn't see Chance enter. He simply appeared beside her in his suit and helped her lift a sculpture with a heavy base. "Where to?"

"The back. There's enough people taking things out front. We'll just get in each other's way."

There was no time for conversation as they rushed to their task. Within minutes all the pieces had been removed from harm's way, and then, mercifully, the flow of water stopped.

"What a mess." Dismayed and dripping, Daisy stood assessing the damage.

Several inches of water puddled on the floor of the empty gallery and trickled into the front room. A berm of canvas cloth that Sean had mounded there protected the front desk and the entrance to the sales gallery.

Still, the floors were a mess and there would be water stains everywhere. Not to mention that big hole in the wall.

"It's the landlord's responsibility to fix this, but the building belongs to the Havershaw Corporation." Daisy groaned. "It'll take weeks to get any action."

"No, it won't. What's the property manager's name and phone number?" In his eagerness to help, Chance seemed oblivious to the way his tie hung crooked and the fact that his shoes and pant cuffs were saturated with dirty water.

"Here." She fetched them for him.

Outside, the crowd of people dissipated. Sean was standing guard over the evacuated sculptures, thanking the people who'd helped him and handing them invitations to Sunday's opening.

A lot of good that would do, Daisy reflected grimly. They'd have to postpone it for sure.

As Chance stood dialing, a striking woman in her thirties entered the gallery. Dressed in a designer suit, with the smoothest honey-blond hair Daisy had ever seen, she stayed on the safe side of the mounded canvas and regarded the displayed paintings with interest.

"I'm afraid we had a bit of a flood," Daisy said.

"This is very high-quality work." The woman held out her hand. "Hi, I'm Gillian Langham. You must be Daisy Redford."

They shook. "Nice to meet you." It seemed like an inane thing to say, but what was the correct greeting for a woman who'd once been engaged to the father of your baby?

Chance spoke clearly and crisply into the phone, outlining the situation in a few sentences and demanding immediate repairs. "As Miss Redford's attorney, I must advise you that any delay could cause further damage to the contents and to the conduct of her business."

Gillian winked at Daisy. "Sometimes it's handy having a lawyer around."

"It would be even handier having a plumber." No sooner had the words left her mouth than she realized they might be taken as a slam against the legal profession, but the other woman merely smiled.

"I see what you mean," Gillian said with a glance at the mess. She nodded toward the fanciful paper works on the sidewalk. "It looks like you got some free advertising, though."

Passersby were stopping to look. Sean, who had fetched an armload of the gallery's brochures, handed them out liberally.

"They say every cloud has a silver lining." Daisy sighed. "I can't believe the timing! One of my best friends, who also happens to be Chance's sister, is getting married this weekend and I've got an exhibit opening on Sunday. This flood is all I needed!"

"Chance's sister is getting married? Which one?"

Daisy had forgotten that Gillian must have met some if not all of Chance's family. "Elise. She's the oldest but the last of the seven to get married."

"Good for her." A trace of wistfulness crossed Gillian's face but vanished so quickly that Daisy thought maybe she'd imagined it.

Chance was still on the phone. He gave Daisy a nod, as if to indicate that progress was being made. She hoped so, although she didn't see how the gallery could be repaired in time for Sunday's event.

Before the silence could lengthen awkwardly, Daisy decided she owed Chance a favor in return. He'd suggested she ask Gillian how families coped with the long hours, so she did.

"How do they cope?" Gillian repeated, straightening her purse on her shoulder. "Well, I understand that the wives formed a support group."

"A support group?" Daisy hoped that wasn't like a therapy group. She might need therapy, but she was going to need practical assistance a lot more.

"They have an emergency baby-sitting exchange, and they organize group outings," the attorney explained.

"In the afternoons?"

"Evenings, too. Sometimes they go to the opera or the ballet together."

"Without their husbands?" She hated to sound naive. "I mean, once in a while would be okay, but not all the time."

"You'll adjust," Gillian said confidently. "Really, Daisy, people who marry lawyers have to give them a break. Even when they're home, they have briefs to prepare."

Chance looked so vibrant and warm right now, conversing on the phone with an air of satisfaction. Daisy tried to picture what it would be like waiting for him to come home every evening, and then having him stagger through the door with an armload of briefs.

It was a different problem than she'd ever expected to face. Daisy's father had simply never been around. She'd never given any thought to the possibility that a person could be physically present but emotionally unavailable.

She wanted the man she knew. The life she knew. If only Chance did, too.

He hung up and joined them. "Have you two introduced yourselves?"

"We have," Gillian said cheerfully, without a trace of possessiveness toward him. Daisy was glad there were no lingering sparks between the two.

But she could see how single-minded the other woman was in pursuing her goal. Which, right now, was to lure Chance to Washington.

"There'll be a repair crew arriving first thing tomorrow," he told Daisy. "They'll have special equipment to dry the place, and the landlord promises they'll fix the wall and replace any damaged flooring."

"You could still sue," Gillian said. "You're going to lose several days' business and some of the sculptures may have been damaged when they were carted out."

"Why should I sue? The accident wasn't the landlord's fault."

"There was a combination of causes," Chance observed, not taking sides in the discussion. "Apparently, the city workers sent a surge of water through an old rusted-out pipe, and it gave way."

"The pipe should have been replaced long ago," Gillian said. "But I was just making a suggestion."

"By the way," Chance told Daisy, "Gillian and I have to go over some specifics about the new family law division tonight. I'll see you tomorrow at the rehearsal dinner, okay?"

"Sure." Daisy had been hoping Chance would say no to the offer at the first meeting. Still, he could hardly refuse to listen to Gillian when she'd flown halfway across the country to see him.

A city crew arrived with materials to soak up the water, and there was no further time for discussion. Daisy managed to thank Chance for his help and tell Gillian how pleasant it had been to meet her, and then they departed.

She and Sean got busy moving the outdoor pieces into the back rooms. Daisy had no further time to think about Chance until she arrived home that night, dirty and weary.

In his absence she showered, fixed herself dinner and stared at the TV. It was just like the old days before she'd met Chance. Lonely and unsatisfying.

She needed him. It didn't matter whether they lived in her condo or in his house. Difficult as it might be for her career, Daisy could even adapt to moving to another area, if it meant having the close-knit family she'd dreamed of.

But she couldn't go to Washington and spend night after night alone. She wouldn't put herself or their child through such an experience.

She had to find a way to fight back, Daisy told herself. She couldn't let Chance go, and her attempts to communicate hadn't worked.

"What I need is a little advice," she said out loud. "Jane Jasmine, what have you got for me?"

In the kitchen, she plucked *2001 Ways to Wed* from the counter and flipped through it. Surely there was a useful nugget of wisdom.

She found it near the end of the book, in a chapter entitled "Resolving Differences." One subsection was called "What Are Friends For?"

"In the old days, people used to depend on go-betweens to woo the object of their affections," the book said.

Sometimes the technique backfired, as anyone knows who's seen *Cyrano de Bergerac* or Shakespeare's *Twelfth Night*. But messengers are a proven method of breaking down barriers.

Even today, go-betweens can help resolve an impasse or overcome stubborn resistance. Sometimes a lover who won't listen to you will listen to someone else.

Even though she often confided in her friends, Daisy hesitated to involve them in such a personal matter. The breach of privacy might only infuriate Chance.

But if she didn't take action, she was going to lose him, anyway. Resolutely Daisy closed the book and went next door to see Elise.

Chapter Fifteen

On Thursday night Chance dreamed that he was about to address the Supreme Court when he discovered he'd prepared for the wrong case.

The chief justice responded to this lapse with fury. Come to think of it, the chief justice looked an awful lot like Daisy.

Then, suddenly, he couldn't find her. He wandered around the halls of justice, asking people if they'd seen Deirdre. They all said they'd never met anyone by that name.

Chance awoke in a sweat, with the covers halfway off the bed and his pillow punched into a ball. He dragged himself to his feet. Big day ahead.

There was an adoption to finalize this morning. And another meeting with Gillian. They had one last session scheduled at lunch on Saturday.

She was, he knew, hoping to get his signature on a preliminary agreement before she left. Chance hated to put her off, which might give her and her superiors an impression of weakness. A topnotch attorney had to be decisive.

As hot water sheeted over his body, he wondered why it should be considered a weakness for him to have a mixed reaction to the firm's offer. After all, the change would be wrenching for Daisy, on top of adjusting to a new baby and, he hoped, a new marriage.

But for him it was the opportunity of a lifetime, his one remaining chance to maximize the talents he'd been blessed with. How could he say no?

NORMALLY, THE WEDDING dinner would have been scheduled to follow the rehearsal, but the minister wasn't available until eight o'clock. And the Foster family claimed their stomachs would rumble like choo-choo trains if they didn't dine until after nine.

So the dinner, an informal affair at Elise's insistence, was scheduled for six o'clock at The Prickly Pear.

"I'd feel disloyal if we held it anywhere else," she'd explained when she invited Daisy and Phoebe. "Besides, my sisters want to bring their kids. How many places would tolerate the noise?"

The place *was* noisy, Daisy discovered when she arrived. The Foster family, with spouses and offspring, practically filled the dining area.

James's side was more modestly represented. His parents had arrived from Tucson and were joined by his brother Bobby and Bobby's fiancée, a pretty young woman named Sandra.

Bill White, whom James had enlisted as a groomsman, attended with Frannie. The couple sat at the bar, joking with Jeff Hawkin and beaming at each other.

Daisy scanned the room for Chance, in vain. His absence made her uneasy.

He hadn't called that afternoon. She'd expected that he would, if he'd made a decision one way or the other about the Washington job. But then, Gillian wasn't leaving until tomorrow afternoon.

Not that Daisy had had time to brood. The repair crew had arrived as promised and done an amazing job of drying out the floors and wall. They'd patched the hole and promised to return tomorrow to repaint and refinish as needed.

Since Daisy was leaving early for the wedding on Saturday, she and Sean would have to rush to set up the DinoCouture exhibit before its Sunday opening. The schedule would be tight, but at least the gallery was usable, thanks to Chance's intervention.

She owed him a big thank-you. But that wasn't going to make it any easier if he announced that he was moving. Because, after long and agonizing consideration, she'd realized she couldn't go with him. If she did, the stress and the loneliness would sooner or later destroy their relationship, and she would be left with neither a husband nor a gallery.

It was too much for him to ask. And too much for her to put herself and her child through.

Still, she hadn't played her last card yet. As long as Chance hadn't signed any binding agreement, Jane Jasmine's advice might yet save both the day and Daisy's heart.

As if reading her mind, Elise winked at her from the head of their table. Phoebe, who was alone tonight with Wyatt tied up at work, gave her a knowing nod. Even Bill, sitting at the bar, gave her a thumbs-up.

Her friends had responded with understanding when Daisy explained how dire the situation was. The only thing she hadn't told them was that she'd decided for sure not to go with Chance.

Giving him an ultimatum might put his back up. She didn't want to use that ammunition unless all else failed.

Tonight during the relaxed dinner seemed the perfect opportunity for her friends to talk sense to Chance. But where was he?

CHANCE WAS IMPRESSED. More than impressed. He would be assistant attorney in charge of the new division on a fast track to a junior partnership in the firm.

That put him near the top of the new division's staff of a dozen lawyers. It was clear that Roker, Sandringham, Wiley and Farrar did things in a big way.

"We'll be second to none," Gillian told him. "We don't want our clients to think we're just adding one or two attorneys as an afterthought."

She showed him the agreement she wanted him to sign. Too suave to pressure him, she simply left it on the table during the meal.

He didn't sign it. But they still had tomorrow.

The meeting ran late, and, instead of leaving the office early as usual on Fridays, Chance played catch-up all afternoon. In the back of his mind he remembered that he had to be at the wedding rehearsal at eight.

Nell stuck her head into his office and said something when she left at five. On the phone, Chance nodded and let her words rattle in his head without really hearing them.

Something about dinner.

He'd been playing phone tag all day with one client, whom he finally reached at six-thirty. When she learned that her estranged husband's latest custody filing contended she was an unfit mother, she was so upset that Chance stayed on the line for over an hour, reassuring her.

By the time he finished, he was starved. He'd forgotten all about dinner, Chance realized.

Dinner. Nell had mentioned it.

Her words rose from the recesses of his memory. "Don't forget the rehearsal dinner. The restaurant has a strange name. I think it's the Broccoli Bear."

The Prickly Pear. Nell didn't usually make mistakes like that about names, but then, she hadn't seen the written invitation, which had arrived at Chance's home.

Then he remembered. The dinner wasn't after the rehearsal but before it. At six o'clock.

It was now seven-thirty. He'd missed eating, obviously. Well, it was his own loss, since he'd have to go hungry until later. As one of the ushers, though, he had an obligation to attend the rehearsal.

No problem, he thought. In this business he was used to skipping meals.

DAISY COULDN'T BRING herself to call Chance. What if he was still with Gillian? She didn't believe there was anything personal going on, but she hated to interrupt.

Finally James got a call on his cellular phone and announced that Chance apologized for missing the dinner. He'd been tied up with a client and would meet them at the church.

Since it was already seven-thirty, that left no time for Daisy's friends to have a heart-to-heart with him. "I can still drop hints," Bill promised, stopping by to commiserate.

"I'll give him a swift kick in the...just kidding," Elise said.

"I'll do worse than that to his 'just kidding' if I get a chance," muttered Phoebe.

So much for her plans, Daisy thought. She almost regretted involving her friends.

Please let him have decided against taking the job. Then none of this will be necessary.

The only bright spot in her evening was Frannie, who bubbled with nervous excitement about her plan to lure the calico cat, whom she'd dubbed Patches, into a carrier and bring him home. She was planning to go at lunchtime tomorrow and made it plain that she could use a little help, since Bill had an appointment with an exterminator to rid Mesa Blue of an ant problem.

No one volunteered. Nell might be available, though, Frannie speculated.

Daisy hoped so. And she was grateful for the mental image of Frannie rescuing a cat, which entertained her en route to the wedding rehearsal.

She forgot about Frannie's escapades, however, as soon as she reached the church. Chance, who had arrived first, stood with the minister in the community hall doorway.

Despite having worked a long day, he looked energized. Dynamic. His back was straight and his eyes sparkled as he laughed at something the pastor said.

Daisy's heart squeezed. She hadn't held him since Tuesday night, and she missed him. How could she possibly go through a lifetime separated from him?

When she first discovered his identity, Daisy had been afraid of losing him to another woman. Instead, she was losing him to himself. To his own ambition.

She didn't want to stand in his way. Or to get trampled as he pursued his dream.

DAISY LOOKED WORRIED, Chance noticed. He hurried forward to take her arm.

"You should be sitting down," he said. "Do you feel all right?"

"I'm fine." She was still frowning, though.

He had to admit he hadn't been as attentive during the pregnancy as he'd planned. After the ultrasound, she'd notified him of several further doctor visits, but they'd conflicted with court hearings. A few back rubs and some solicitous questions had so far been Chance's major contribution to her well-being.

"You're not having any health problems?" he probed. "The flood cleanup must have kept you on your feet all day."

"I didn't have to do much. I mostly stayed out of the crew's way." Her expression softened. "Thanks for calling the property manager. You have a magic touch."

"Do you need help mounting the exhibit on Sunday?" he asked. "I'll be there if you need me."

"You spend Sunday mornings with your family."

"You're my family now," he said. "You and the baby." She winced, as if he'd said something painful. "Are you sure you're okay? You're not having premature contractions, are you?"

She was shaking her head when Bill arrived. "They want us groomsmen in the back," he said.

Reluctantly Chance surrendered Daisy to Phoebe, who for some reason regarded him sternly. If he'd drawn disapproval from his sister, he would have understood, because he'd missed her rehearsal dinner. What was Phoebe mad about?

Women. With seven sisters, Chance ought to understand them by now. But he sure didn't.

At the back of the hall, the minister explained to the best man and the two groomsmen about their duties and the procedure. How to seat ladies. Where to put family members. Chance, having been involved in several of his sisters' ceremonies, already knew the routine.

Afterward, as they waited for the run-through, Bill said, "I wonder if you've given any thought to what I told you."

Chance searched his memory and came up blank. "Told me about what?"

"About sometimes needing to let the woman take the lead," he said.

"No, we're supposed to take her arm and escort her," Chance corrected.

"I meant, like Frannie and me," Bill said earnestly. "And the cats."

He was obviously trying to make a point, but Chance couldn't grasp it. "I told Daisy she could name our cat, if we ever get one. I believe we settled on Tom or Kitty."

"That wasn't..."

James's brother Bobby came by. "I hate to break in, but we're supposed to take our places."

Chance followed him around the back of the hall. As he went by his sister, who was waiting with their father, he said, "I'm sorry about missing the dinner, 'Lise. If it's any consolation, I'm ravenous."

"I'll talk to you later," she growled.

He stopped. "About what?"

"Daisy."

A warning bell rang in the back of his mind. "What do you mean, you'll talk to me about Daisy?"

"You want to hear it now? Okay. In a nutshell, I think you're indulging yourself at her expense," Elise said, flaring.

Chance didn't get the point until Sam said, "Son, I

think the ladies are unhappy that you might be moving to Washington.''

"They've been talking about me?" he asked, annoyed. He didn't like having his personal business the subject of gossip, even among his own family members.

"You mean Daisy can't talk about her problems to her best friends?" Elise said. "I knew you were overbearing, but this is ridiculous.''

Finding it impossible to frame a dignified answer, Chance strode in Bobby's wake. Inside, however, he churned with an irritation intensified by hunger.

So Daisy had been talking to her friends about her "problems," which apparently included him. If she had objections to his plans, she should tell him directly.

Now he understood what Bill had been hinting at when he mentioned letting the woman lead. Daisy must have enlisted him, too, in some kind of campaign to change Chance's mind.

This went beyond her family and most intimate friends. It bordered on betrayal.

PACING DOWN the makeshift aisle, clutching a bouquet of paper flowers, Daisy saw Chance standing between Bobby and Bill. His jaw worked, and his eyes narrowed as he studied her.

His anger was clearly directed at her, although she wasn't sure what she'd done to provoke it. Tears stung inside her lids, and her mock bouquet trembled in her hands.

Darn it, she loved Chance. She didn't want to fight with him.

When Daisy had dreamed of falling in love and having a child, she'd never imagined suffering such heartache. If this were true love, shouldn't it triumph over everything?

She hoped she was wrong and that his fury was directed at someone else. That hope withered a few minutes later when, immediately after the mock ceremony, he took her arm and led her aside.

"We need to talk," he said grimly.

"I guess we do."

They reached a secluded corner. "I don't appreciate having you discuss our private concerns with other people." Chance kept his voice low and close to her ear.

"I always talk things over with my closest friends." Daisy struggled to keep her voice steady. "I rely on their advice to keep me from flying off half-cocked."

"Is Bill one of your closest friends?" he demanded.

"What did he say?" She couldn't imagine the mild-mannered superintendent giving offense.

"It isn't so much what he said as the fact that he said anything," Chance snarled. "This is none of his business."

She had to make him understand. Tomorrow he would see Gillian for the last time and, most likely, make his decision. "I was trying to find a way to reach you."

"I'm right here," he said tightly. "You can talk to me anytime you want."

"No, I can't!"

"You can if you want to."

Every instinct dating back to her fatherless childhood and two failed relationships prepared Daisy for either a big fight or complete silence. The end of everything.

She refused to panic. If Chance wanted to talk, she'd

try. "I have roots here in Phoenix. They can't just be ripped up and replanted somewhere else."

"Nobody said it would be easy." With his shoulder he shielded the two of them. A couple of people glanced their way but, seeing a private tête-à-tête, turned away.

"I'm willing to meet you halfway," Daisy said. "Maybe more than halfway. But you're asking me to give up my career for a husband who'll never be around."

"You won't be giving up your career. And you'd see more of me in Washington when we're married than you do now," he insisted.

She hated having this conversation under these circumstances. They ought to be sitting quietly in her condo, or at his house. "Why don't we go somewhere else?"

"You can't refute what I'm saying, so you're putting me off. Is that it?" Chance demanded.

"No!"

"I haven't eaten and I need to review the contract Gillian gave me," he said. "If you have a point to make, make it now."

"It isn't that simple!"

"It would be simpler if you had a rational argument. Instead, you're letting your emotions run away with you," Chance said. "I wouldn't do anything to harm you or our child. Why can't you trust me?"

He was asking her to put her future in his hands. To let him make the decisions and to rely on his good intentions.

Daisy didn't doubt that Chance meant well. He wasn't trying to take advantage of her. But when he stubbornly refused to see her point of view, how could she yield?

"Why can't you trust *me?*" she asked. "And I'm not being irrational!"

To her frustration, tears streamed down her cheeks. *Oh, great. He'll take that as a sign that I've completely lost control.* And maybe she had.

Chance released an exasperated breath. "I didn't mean to distress you. But you're going to have to accept that I know what I'm doing, and that it will work out for the best. Now we both need to get a good night's sleep."

Daisy wiped away a tear and struggled to find some way to explain what she meant. But she'd already done her best. "I wish you'd listen."

"And I wish you'd stop making everything out to be my fault," he said. "I did listen, Daisy. I'll always listen. Can you get home all right?"

"I can drive," she said, and couldn't resist adding, "in spite of my irrational state."

As he walked away, utter misery settled over her. He'd made it clear that his mind was made up. He intended to accept the job.

She'd done everything she could think of, including enlisting her friends to try to talk sense to Chance. Not only hadn't the effort worked, it had backfired.

She'd lost him.

As HE EXITED the church hall, Chance wished he didn't feel so guilty. The sight of Daisy's tears wrenched him. He'd heard that pregnancy wreaked havoc with a woman's emotions, but he knew he was partly responsible, too.

Well, he'd tried once again to hear her out, hadn't

he? She was overreacting to his job offer the same way she'd overreacted when she'd seen him driving Lanie to court.

Jumping to false conclusions. Failing to look at all the evidence.

Of course, in Lanie's case, Daisy had come to his office and resolved the matter. He was still trying to figure out why, this time, she refused to grasp the big picture, when he saw Phoebe standing next to his car with storm clouds in her eyes.

"Waiting for me?" he asked in weary resignation.

"You bet I am!" The woman's steely fury belied her china-doll blond looks. "I want to talk to you about Daisy."

"Anything I have to say, I've already said to her." He couldn't open the driver's door without bumping her, so Chance waited, not very patiently.

"Yes, I saw you two talking," she said. "Or rather, I saw her trying to talk and you making her cry."

Her analysis didn't soften his sense of guilt one iota. "Maybe that's how it looked to you, but believe me, there are no problems that Daisy and I can't work out."

"Are you determined to move?"

"I haven't committed myself. It looks that way, though," he said. "Believe me, I've listened to all Daisy's arguments."

"You were only listening in order to frame your answers."

He didn't want to be rude, but on the other hand her prying was unwarranted. "Could you step aside, please?"

Phoebe ignored his request. "Here she has the opportunity of a lifetime. Maybe you don't realize what it will mean if her one-woman show is part of the gallery tour, but believe me, it's a big deal.''

"Excuse me?" He hated to admit to ignorance about what appeared to be an important development in Daisy's life. "What gallery tour?"

"The Arizona Craft Arts Association is sponsoring an international symposium next spring," Phoebe said. "Didn't she tell you the president of the association bought one of her pots and wants to include her show?"

"No," Chance admitted. "When did this happen?"

Phoebe twisted a length of blond hair around one finger. "That's right, I forgot. It was the same day you found out about your job offer."

"She should have told me."

"She said she didn't think it would make any difference," said Daisy's friend. "You dismissed everything she said. Exactly like you were doing a few minutes ago."

"You couldn't have heard what we said!"

"No, but as a former actress I know a lot about body language," she said. "You were cross-examining her. Why would she bring up something as important as her exhibit so you could treat it as simply another point to attack?"

"I wouldn't have done that," he said.

Phoebe regarded him coolly. "Are you sure?" She stepped away from his car. "Well, I've had my say. You can heed it or not, as you choose."

Chance released the locks by remote control and got inside, his brain in a whirl. So Daisy hadn't told him about an important career opportunity here in Phoenix.

How could he weigh all the facts if she withheld something so important?

You were cross-examining her. Was that true?

Phoebe's words rang in his ears all the way home.

Chapter Sixteen

On Saturday morning Daisy and Sean mounted the DinoCouture show. Thanks to careful planning, they finished before lunchtime.

Daisy and Phoebe had agreed to meet at Elise's condo at 2:00 p.m. to dress, apply makeup and fix their hair together. A limousine would arrive at 3:15 to take them to the church.

Too restless to hang around the gallery until then, Daisy turned it over to Sean. On her way home she grabbed a bite to eat and then, impulsively, stopped near the alley where the feral cat colony lived.

Frannie's dented station wagon was parked by the curb. Daisy paused, wondering if this was a good idea.

The presence of too many people might frighten Patches. But Frannie had asked for moral support.

Besides, Daisy had hovered on the verge of tears all morning. She didn't want to spend the next two hours crying and show up with a ruined face for Elise's wedding. Better to involve herself in something.

As she started down the alley, Daisy remembered the night she'd come here with Chance. What a delightful adventure, and only one of many. When they were together, every experience was exciting.

She'd never felt so at ease with a man before. He'd become a friend and more.

Until he received the job offer from Washington. In the past week he'd grown distant and arbitrary. She wanted things back the way they were.

She needed Chance. Needed his smile and his strong embrace and his warmth. She missed the teasing between them. But when would they have time for that, even if she did go with him?

Ahead she spotted the red-haired woman crouching by a small hard-plastic cage with a handle. Her lime-green sweatpants and green-and-yellow knit top blazed brighter than the early-September sunshine.

Frannie caught her eye and nodded toward the cat carrier, which stood open. The plan, Daisy recalled, was to provide a can of delicious-smelling salmon and lure Patches inside.

Other cats circled nearby, meowing warily. Being wild, however, none of them dared come too close to a human.

Except for the calico. He approached Frannie, meowed and rolled over. When she reached to pat him, he tolerated it for a moment, then jumped back fearfully.

Patches wanted love, Daisy thought, but he feared it, too. No doubt he'd been hurt before.

I am not going to make parallels between myself and that cat! I'm not afraid of love. But maybe Chance is.

The insight startled her. How could such a popular, confident man be afraid of getting hurt? He was, after all, the one who'd pursued her, especially since he'd learned about the pregnancy.

But he didn't trust their relationship enough to make it the focus of his life, the way he expected her to do.

He was hedging his bets, wanting to keep her on the sidelines while pursuing his career one hundred percent.

That was what men traditionally did. But it was only fair that he, like Daisy, should balance his work with the demands of parenthood and marriage. And the demands of marriage included making room for the other person's career.

She sighed. She'd learned a tremendous amount in the months she'd spent with Chance, about herself and him and how to get along with a life partner.

The one thing she hadn't learned was how to share this newfound wisdom with the man she loved.

Patches came forward again and sniffed the carrier. "He doesn't seem afraid of it, just cautious," Frannie said softly.

"How are you going to keep him from running away once you get him home?" Daisy asked, careful to keep her distance from the cat because of the risk to her baby.

"I'll have to keep him indoors for a while," Frannie said. "I'm not looking forward to the litter box training, although some cats take to it fast."

Patches stuck his head inside the carrier. The smell of fish must have overruled his qualms because he advanced inside.

"Shoot. One leg and his tail are still sticking out," Frannie muttered.

"Couldn't you push him?"

"Cats are like greased lightning. Once he gets alarmed, he'll be gone, and next time he'll avoid the carrier," she said.

"You sound like the voice of experience," Daisy said.

The cat lady nodded. "I often have to take my cats to the vet, so they come to associate the carrier with pain. If I can't stuff them inside, I have to get a knockout pill, but the vets don't dispense them without good reason."

"I wish they made a knockout pill for men," Daisy muttered. "A legal one, I mean!"

"To immobilize them just long enough for, say, a certain Washington lawyer to get herself back on the plane?" Frannie asked.

"Don't remind me." Right now Chance must be sitting at a table with Gillian, possibly signing away their happiness. "The worst thing is, I believe he's going to make himself miserable. Even if I go along with him, I don't believe he'll be happy at that job for long."

"I thought he'd wanted this opportunity for years." Frannie kept a close eye on Patches, whose leg and tail were still sticking out.

"He used to want it but he let it go," Daisy said. "Now that it's been thrust under his nose, though, he can't resist the temptation. Maybe he'll enjoy the challenge at first, but I think he'll get tired of not having a life."

"I hope he comes to his senses before he throws away something precious," Frannie said thoughtfully. Suddenly a grin spread across her face. "Gotcha!"

The cat had shifted position and moved its bottom farther inside the carrier. Swiftly Frannie latched the metal wire door.

There was no immediate reaction. Busy eating, Patches didn't notice he was trapped.

A moment later he began turning anxiously, thumping the sides of the carrier. A pitiful meowing issued from his furry throat.

"Poor little guy," Frannie said. "It's okay, Patches. I'm going to take you home now."

"Won't he be angry with you?" Daisy asked as Frannie lifted the carrier.

"Cats are very forgiving," she said. "Besides, I didn't force him in, so he may not be sure he didn't somehow get himself stuck in the cage."

"You've got quite a job ahead of you." Daisy walked alongside her friend toward their cars. In the midday heat and with her growing girth, she was grateful for their deliberate pace.

The carrier swayed as Patches protested this unaccustomed means of travel. His little cries, not unlike a baby's, made Daisy's heart go out to him.

"You know, most of us can't save the world," Frannie said. "We can make a little piece of it better, though. And this is my way of doing so."

Instinctively Daisy's hand went to her abdomen. She would do her best to make this corner of the world a bit better, too, for her child—with or without Chance.

"THERE MAY BE A PROBLEM with my wife. Future wife," Chance said.

"Oh?" Gillian's blond hair bounced as she slanted him a questioning look.

"Not a problem exactly," he amended. "She may need to keep her gallery open here in Phoenix for a while. So I suppose we'll have to have a long-distance relationship at first."

It was the best solution Chance had come up with. Phoebe's words had disturbed him, and last night, tossing and turning sleeplessly, he'd sought a way to be fair to Daisy.

"What about the baby?" Gillian asked. "Won't that complicate matters?"

"Both grandmothers can help out," Chance said.

Gillian waved away a hovering waiter. "I'll be honest with you. At Roker, Sandringham, Wiley and Farrar, there simply isn't the time or energy for marital complications."

He couldn't believe he'd heard her correctly. "Every firm has employees who suffer marital problems at some point."

"We discourage them." Gillian didn't seem to grasp how outrageous that sounded. "We've found it works best if either the couple is childless and the spouse also works long hours, or if the wife is home full-time and can give her husband complete support."

Uneasily Chance recalled his promise that Daisy wouldn't have to compromise her career. He'd brushed aside her argument that it would be difficult, especially in a new place, with a new baby.

He'd told her to trust him. Maybe she'd been wise not to.

In keeping with the theme of A Garden Party, the church sanctuary had been transformed. Guests entered through a rose-covered trellis and sat surrounded by a flowering fantasy garden in dark-green and two shades of pink.

Daisy barely caught a glimpse before she, Elise and Phoebe were spirited by the bride's mother to a cloak room where they could wait unseen. She buried her nose in her bouquet and tried hard to forget everything except wishing for her friend's happiness.

The photographer came in and posed them, taking a variety of shots. Daisy did her best to smile.

"A Garden Party. It's so beautiful, I wish I'd chosen the theme first!" Phoebe sighed after he left.

"But you picked a great theme, too. Life Is a Rainbow gives you so much scope, especially given your famous color sense," teased Elise, adjusting a circlet of rosebuds atop her light-brown hair.

"Be careful!" said her mother. "Let me fix the curls." She poked at what appeared to Daisy to be a perfect coiffeur. Fussing was Margaret Foster's way of calming her own nerves.

"Did you happen to talk to Chance last night?" Phoebe asked Daisy.

"No, why?"

"I would have asked you earlier, but I was waiting for you to mention it." Staring into a hand mirror, the blond woman touched up her lipstick. "I gave him a piece of my mind right before he left the rehearsal. Maybe I shouldn't have."

Daisy shrugged. "I don't suppose it did any harm. Things couldn't get much worse."

"Oh, dear," Margaret said. "I knew there would be trouble when he told us about this job offer. I even suggested the two of you get counseling."

"What did he say?"

"He said you both had good communication skills and you could work it out." Chance's mother sighed. "He's stubborn and strong willed. Always was, even as a child."

It made Daisy feel better to find her potential future mother-in-law sympathetic. On the other hand, if Margaret couldn't influence her son, who could?

"Oh, listen," Elise said. "I want to ask you two about my bouquet."

Both women regarded the charming spray of deep-

and dusty-pink flowers against dark-green foliage. "It's splendid," Phoebe pronounced.

"I wasn't asking for your opinion of it," said the bride. "I meant about throwing it afterward."

"Try not to hit anybody in the face," her mother said.

"Mom! There's nothing wrong with my aim." Elise sounded more like a teenager than a college professor. "I meant, to whom should I throw it?"

"It's supposed to go to the next woman to be married," her mother reminded her.

"Aren't you supposed to toss it blindly into the air?" Daisy asked. "And let fate decide who the lucky girl is?"

"Nobody does that," Elise said. "It's always rigged."

"That doesn't seem right," Phoebe said.

Elise glared at her. "I do want to ask your opinions *if* you can bring yourselves to listen for a minute."

"We're listening," Phoebe said.

"Okay. So, everybody knows your wedding is next month," Elise said. "And of course Frannie is going to be married soon, too. But what's the point in bestowing fate's blessing on someone who's already got the guy signed, sealed and delivered?"

"You aren't bestowing fate's blessing," Daisy pointed out. "If you rig the results, you're only bestowing your own blessing."

"As the bride, I am temporarily possessed of magic powers," her friend countered. "And I want to throw the bouquet to you, if I can restrain myself from beating my brother about the ears with it."

"Don't waste those beautiful flowers on Chance," Phoebe said.

"You wouldn't be offended if I don't aim it at you?"

"Not at all."

"Daisy? What do you think?"

That was a tricky question. Chance resented Daisy's discussing their personal situation with anyone else, and he might interpret this use of the very public bouquet tradition as yet another sign that she was maneuvering behind his back.

The heck with it. She was tired of trying to second-guess him. "I'd love to have the flowers if you promise to forgive me in case I decide not to marry your brother."

Margaret clasped her hands together. "I hope it doesn't come to that."

"It won't. As I said, I have magic powers today." Elise smiled as her father peeked through the door. "Is it time already?"

Sam nodded. "You know, I've done this six times before, and every time I get all choked up about losing my little girl. Are you sure you're ready to be married?"

"Dad! I'm thirty-three years old!"

"Just asking," he said, and offered his arm.

As Daisy walked down the aisle beside Phoebe, she could see surprised expressions at the side-by-side arrangement. But no one seemed displeased.

There were guests she didn't recognize, probably friends of James's and people Elise knew from work. And many familiar faces, too: Helen and Rolland Madison, holding hands as they sat with Wyatt. Jeff Hawkin, patting Frannie's arm as she wept happy tears.

Elise's sisters formed a large contingent with their

husbands and children. Some sobbed openly, others nodded with contentment. No matter how familiar the experience of a wedding, it never grew old.

Finally she dared look ahead to the altar, where James stood glowing with anticipation beside the pastor. His brother wore a satisfied smile, while Bill was winking at Frannie.

Her gaze was drawn, inexorably, to the man standing between Bobby and Bill. Chance.

If only she could interpret that solemn expression! If only he would at least meet her gaze.

In the elegant tuxedo, he was almost unbearably handsome. And remote. The gray eyes, which in moments of warmth turned iridescent, now glittered cold as ice.

Did he sign the job agreement?

He should have called to tell her the news earlier. One way or the other.

Her mind hurried to make excuses. Perhaps he'd been too rushed. If the meeting with Gillian had run long, he'd have been racing to get to the church on time.

Or maybe he didn't want to tell her. Maybe he was already shutting her out of his life.

Daisy clutched her spray of flowers. Was he even now planning how to break the bad news?

She didn't want to fight with him in front of his family. It would be best if they postponed their discussion until later this evening.

If only her nerves could stand the strain.

She and Phoebe reached the front. By prior arrangement Phoebe stood closest to the altar. In her enlarged state Daisy preferred to be as far from the center of attention as possible.

The organ music swelled, and here came the bride. In her white gown, Elise had a gossamer, otherworldly quality as if she really might possess magic powers.

"I'm glad she didn't wear lime-green," Phoebe murmured.

Daisy stifled a giggle.

AFTERWARD EVERYONE agreed the ceremony had been perfect. True, James's housekeeper sobbed so loudly in the second row that she drowned out some of the pastor's words. And the photographer dropped a film can with an audible *plunk!* just as James put the ring on Elise's finger. But those incidents only added to the memories.

The joyous couple departed for the reception in a limousine. Another limo carried the bridesmaids, best man and groomsmen. Chance spent the whole ride gazing out the window.

It was not a good sign, Daisy thought glumly.

In the receiving line she noticed several young women lingering to flirt with him. He looked so striking in his tuxedo that she couldn't blame them, but the sight was hardly reassuring.

His playboy reputation hadn't been entirely unearned. Women flocked to him. If she let him go to Washington without her, he wouldn't be alone for long.

He'd only offered marriage after he learned that she was pregnant, she reflected. Maybe she'd mistaken the depth of his feelings all along. Maybe he wasn't willing to compromise because losing her would only hurt him a little.

Daisy brushed away a tear. "Weddings are so emotional," she said by way of explanation to Helen Madison, who was waiting to give her regards to the bride and groom.

"I plan to bring a whole stack of hankies to Wyatt and Phoebe's!" agreed her neighbor. "I can't wait!"

At last the guests finished their greetings and drifted to the tables set for dinner. In a corner of the room the band played background music.

It was time to eat. For once, though, Daisy lacked her usual appetite.

"IT'S TIME!" Frannie tapped her on the shoulder.

Roused from a reverie, Daisy gave a little jump. The movement rattled the plate holding the remains of her slice of wedding cake. "Time for what?"

"The bouquet!" said the cat lady. "Elise said to tell you she's changing into her traveling suit, and she's going to throw it from the main staircase. She wants you to be there."

"Thanks." Carefully Daisy got up. She was feeling the weight of her pregnancy today, although at five months she only showed a little.

The reception, lovely as it was, had tested her willpower. It took a lot of energy to keep up a cheerful facade while Chance ignored her.

He'd sat at the far end of the head table, conversing with James, Bobby and Bill. He'd danced once with the bride and once with his mother. Not with anyone else.

Daisy told herself it was Chance's restraint about personal matters that made him avoid her. He didn't want to risk a quarrel, or even a warm reconciliation, with so many people watching.

At least she hoped that was the explanation.

With Frannie, Phoebe and a group of other single

women, she adjourned to the hotel lobby. They grouped below an old-fashioned staircase that curved from the mezzanine level.

Behind them trailed a few men, no doubt powered by curiosity. Daisy was acutely aware when Chance appeared, talking with Bill.

Apprehension crept over her. She'd figured Chance might hear about her catching the flowers, but hadn't expected him to be breathing down her neck when Elise threw the bouquet directly at her.

He might make a Federal case out of it. She could never tell, with Chance.

"I wish he'd go away!" she whispered to Phoebe.

"Why? He's been staring at you all evening," said her friend.

"He has?"

"You didn't notice?"

"I didn't think he looked at me at all!"

"He kept glancing away as soon as you turned in his direction," Phoebe assured her.

"You're making this up."

"No, she's not," said Frannie. "I noticed it, too."

"Where's Elise, anyway?" Phoebe asked.

Everyone stared upward, waiting for the bride to appear. There was no movement at the head of the stairs.

"She probably went to the bathroom," someone said after a minute.

"Gee, that reminds me, I need to go, too," said the woman beside her.

"You have to be reminded?"

"I didn't mean it that way!"

Daisy peeked from the corner of her eye. Chance was standing too far away to overhear anything she and her friends might discuss, thank goodness.

"Did he say anything to Bill about whether he accepted the job offer?" she asked Frannie.

The cat lady shook her head. "Not as far as I've heard. I'm sure you'll be the first to know."

"Gillian is the first to know." Daisy sighed. "I mean, since she offered him the job, that makes sense. I just wish he'd taken the time to break the news before the ceremony."

"He was late getting here," Frannie said. "Bill went out in the parking lot to look for him. He said he had to make an important stop on the way."

"More important than being on time to his sister's wedding?" Phoebe sniffed.

"Maybe *he* had to go to the bathroom," Daisy said. They chuckled.

A murmur in the small crowd drew her attention upward. There stood Elise, radiant on James's arm. She'd changed into a tan dress with black piping for their honeymoon flight to Hawaii.

"What a wonderful dress," Phoebe said.

"Not my style, but it does look terrific on her," Frannie agreed.

Daisy was too nervous to speak.

Leaning over the railing, Elise mouthed something at her. It looked like, "Back up."

Other women were clustering so close, Daisy realized, that one of the taller ones was sure to grab the bouquet before it reached her. That suited her fine, but the bride was making it clear she wouldn't release the flowers until she had a clear shot.

The last thing Daisy wanted was an uncomfortable delay, so, obediently, she stepped backward. With a nod Elise posed dramatically, waved her nosegay in the air and tossed it straight at Daisy.

For one rebellious moment, she considered not catching it. But that might spoil her friend's special day, so Daisy dutifully reached for the cluster.

It never got there. At the last minute an arm stretched over her head and snared it.

A gasp went up from the onlookers. *That was rude,* Daisy thought, and turned to see who had stolen the bride's flowers.

It was Chance.

Chapter Seventeen

"Good catch," said Bill, who didn't seem to see anything wrong with a groomsman snagging the bouquet.

"We're not playing baseball," Elise called from her vantage point. "Throw it back up here and I'll try again."

"I caught it fair and square," said her brother. Something in his voice must have put his sister on her guard, because she didn't argue.

Daisy regarded him warily. He'd brushed against her as he reached upward, nearly knocking her over. Although she was certain that hadn't been intentional, he'd better have a good explanation.

She still couldn't read the expression on Chance's face, not because it was blank but because so many emotions tugged at it. A shade of embarrassment, which was well deserved. A bit of smugness. And a trace of—could that be fear?

Despite the indignant chattering of the other women, she didn't think he was afraid of being pounded to death by a group of bouquet-deprived damsels. Obviously, Chance had some trick up his sleeve that he was worried might backfire.

"By tradition these flowers go to the next woman to

marry.'' His firm voice hushed the muttering. "Perhaps I ought to give it to Phoebe or Frannie, but I don't think the rule applies to someone who's already made plans."

Elise nodded in agreement, then stopped and shot her brother a slit-eyed warning look.

"As a lawyer I've consulted my reference books but haven't been able to find a precedent," he went on. "However, I've asked a couple of expert advisers—the best man and my fellow groomsman—and we believe the bouquet rightfully belongs to the next woman to get engaged."

Daisy wondered why a couple of bachelors qualified as expert advisers on such a matter. At the moment, however, she didn't care.

"I'm known for disliking public displays of sentiment," Chance went on, calmly addressing the curious onlookers, who included some stray hotel guests. "It isn't easy for me to take a public risk, but then, I guess it isn't easy for anybody."

"Could you hurry it up?" said a woman. "My friend here has to go to the bathroom."

"Oh, shut up," said her friend. "I wouldn't miss this for the world."

And then Chance did the last thing Daisy would ever have expected. In fact, she would have bet good money against it.

He knelt in front of her. "So I'm presenting these to Daisy in the hope that she'll consent to be my wife. Deirdre Redford, will you marry me?"

Numbly she took the flowers he thrust into her hands. Was this a stunt? And how could she say yes when she didn't know what choice he'd made about Washington?

It didn't seem right to give a qualified answer. *I'll marry you if...* She loved him, but that wouldn't be enough to sustain a marriage unless he loved her just as much.

"I can see the flowers aren't cutting it, so I'm prepared to sweeten the deal." Chance reached into his breast pocket and produced a velvet jeweler's box. He opened it to reveal a gold ring glittering with diamonds. "Of course, you're free to exchange it, but I wanted to give you the general idea."

"If she says no, can I accept?" asked one of the women observers.

"I'm sorry, this is a restricted offer," Chance said. To Daisy he added, "I'm hoping we can tie the knot before Christmas. That way you'll have plenty of time to settle into my house before the baby comes."

"Your house?" she asked. "Your house here in Phoenix?"

"It's the only one I've got," he said. "And the only one I want. Unless you don't like it."

He wasn't going to Washington! "I love it!" Daisy said.

"You love my house?"

"Well, sure. It's beautiful," she said.

Chance cleared his throat. "I don't mean to rush you, but I may need a knee transplant if you don't give me an answer soon."

"Say yes," said Frannie.

"He deserves to suffer, but not too much," agreed Phoebe.

Daisy's throat was so thick with emotion that she couldn't speak. She could hardly believe her dream was coming true.

Chance loved her and intended to stay with her. They were going to be a family.

"The truth is, I don't want to miss spending time with you or seeing our child grow up while I'm off working," he said. "I had one last shot at an old dream, and I needed the freedom to weigh it, but it came up short. The reality would have made us both unhappy."

"I can't believe my brother is admitting he was wrong," Elise said from the stairs. "He never does that!"

"This may be the only time I do, at least publicly, so enjoy it," Chance returned.

Daisy lifted the ring from the box. "Put it on me," she said.

His eyes shining at the implied consent, he slipped the ring onto the third finger of her left hand. "It's a little loose."

"That's okay. I hear pregnant women get puffy." Daisy couldn't restrain herself any longer. Impishly she said, "Oh, by the way, the answer is yes."

"'By the way'?" Chance repeated, lifting one eyebrow.

"After you ignored me all evening, what more do you expect?" she teased.

"She said yes," Phoebe said.

"You can get up now." Frannie gazed worriedly at Chance's knee.

"I want more than a half-hearted yes. I want a great big 'I can't wait!'" He stood and in one swift motion lifted Daisy horizontally in his arms. Like a bride to be carried over the threshold.

"Hey!" She caught his shoulder to steady herself. "What are you doing?"

"Sweeping you off your feet," he said.

Daisy felt silly, suspended in midair. "Yes!" she said. "Okay? Isn't that what you wanted to hear? You can put me down now."

"Louder!"

"Yes, sir!"

"Good enough." Instead of setting her on her feet, though, he whisked her down a carpeted hallway to the cheers and scattered applause of the onlookers.

"Where are we going?" Daisy asked as the noise faded behind them.

"Don't worry. I've got this all planned."

"Don't tell me you booked a room!" she said.

"I wish I'd thought of it." Chance carried her into an elevator and pushed the button for the mezzanine. "Actually, I'm only planning about thirty seconds ahead of my actions. But I'll bet we can find an empty conference room."

Daisy nestled against him. "You know, I kind of envy you," she said.

"Why?"

"Because you get to carry our baby in your arms before I do."

Chance grinned. "I hadn't thought of it that way."

At the mezzanine level, he found a vacant room set up for what appeared to be another wedding reception, although smaller than Elise's. Puffed paper swans topped the tables while two large swans, cut out of cardboard and decorated with white feathers, nuzzled each other in front of the head table.

"I wonder if this means the bride was an ugly duckling," he said as he eased Daisy into a chair.

"I think it means she found Prince Charming, like a princess in a fairy tale," she said.

"Did you?" Chance asked as he sat beside her. "Did you find Prince Charming?"

Daisy nodded and, to her dismay, burst into tears.

"Well, there's a vote of confidence," he teased as he kissed away a tear.

"You don't know how hard this has been," she said. "I thought you were leaving."

"I'm sorry." Chance sighed. "You were right when you called me bossy and arrogant."

"I didn't put it quite that baldly," she protested.

"Well, you should have." He gazed tenderly at her. "Daisy, all along I believed you were the one who needed to get in touch with your feelings. Now I realize it was me, too."

"You'd had that dream for a long time," she said. "About making it big. I can't blame you for not rejecting the opportunity out of hand."

"But I should have considered your reservations instead of dismissing them," he said. "If I had, I might have seen the truth sooner. This morning as I listened to Gillian, I realized that her law firm practically owns its employees. I wouldn't have had much of a private life."

"Even so," she said, "are you sure you won't regret this? I don't want you looking back over the years and wishing for what might have been."

Moisture raised glints of violet in Chance's gray eyes. "I'd never do that. I love you, Daisy, and I love our baby even if I don't know yet whether it's a Tom or a Kitty. The only thing I would ever regret is reaching old age without having spent enough time with you."

She stroked his cheek. "There's no danger of that now."

He smiled. "You know, it's been quite a while since I stayed over at your place."

"Decades and decades," she said.

"Now that we're engaged, I think I should stay there every night."

"Or I could move in with you." Daisy smiled dreamily. "Now that we know it's going to be our home and our child's home, I'd like to start building my nest. What do you think of a Christmas Eve wedding?"

"I'll tell you what." Chance pulled her to her feet. "Let's go back to your place and discuss this in more detail."

"Okay." She was surprised when her pumps touched the floor. She'd assumed, given her mood, that she would float.

"By the way," added her fiancé. "Isn't there something you wanted to mention?"

They slipped out of the room. "About what?"

"A one-woman show in May."

"Oh!" she said. "Yes, I'm having one. Who told you?"

"Someone who cares about you," he said. "Come on, sweetheart. I want to show you exactly how much *I* care about you."

"That sounds like the second-best idea I've heard all night," she said.

"What was the best?"

"Getting married," she said.

ON SUNDAY AFTERNOON not only was the DinoCouture show ready in plenty of time for the opening, but the gallery itself had never looked better. "It needed a good washing," joked Sean as he set out a tray of cheese and crackers.

"A fresh coat of paint never hurts, either." In the front window, Chance finished hanging a paper banner that Daisy had cut in the shape of a boat and lettered this morning.

It said, Reopened after Flood. Come See Our Dinosaurs!

"I like the boat idea," Sean said.

"I was trying to make a reference to Noah's Ark," Daisy explained. "I hope the customers get it."

"If they don't, they can always come inside and ask you to explain it." Chance cleared his tools out of the window recess.

"Bring on the world! After all, we're opening a show and my boss just got engaged!" Sean had been thrilled to learn Daisy wasn't moving to Washington, although he was too polite to make a point of it in front of Chance.

The DinoCouture artist, Elroy McGinnis, arrived a short time later. A small, wiry man in his midthirties with frizzy blond hair, he brought along a friend named Griffin Rale. Although Griffin was sturdier, older and darker in coloring, the two mirrored each others' expressions.

"It's fabulous!" Elroy declared as he surveyed the exhibit.

"What luck, to capitalize on the gallery's renovation!" Griffin said.

"I mean, the place practically sparkles!"

"It's a good omen!"

Daisy didn't think she'd ever before heard so much enthusiasm prior to an opening. Usually the artist was so jittery he or she hardly said a word.

By two o'clock, the time stated on the invitations, guests began arriving. The flood at the gallery and the quick repair job had been reported in the newspaper, accompanied by a photograph of one of Elroy's dinosaurs.

As a result, quite a few newcomers appeared. Daisy welcomed them and added their names to her mailing list.

Arturo Alonzo came with his wife, Bea. "I couldn't wait to meet you," she said, shaking hands with Daisy. "I love the pot he bought! We put it right in the living room."

Daisy introduced them to Chance. "We just got engaged yesterday," she said.

"Congratulations," the older man said. "You're marrying a very talented woman."

"She's someone special," Chance agreed.

"She's going to make a name for herself," Bea added.

"That sounds good to me." He grinned. "Daisy Redford Foster. Does that mean I get a little bit of fame, too?"

"You bet," she said.

Chance didn't seem to mind that the spotlight was on her, Daisy noticed. She'd found a wonderful, generous man.

During a quiet moment, Arturo drew Daisy aside. "The arts committee met on Friday. Ione and I strongly recommended your work, and the photographs were a hit. The vote was unanimous to include your show on the gallery tour."

"Thank you!" she said. "That's wonderful."

"We're always glad to discover fresh talent." Arturo's wife caught his eye, and he excused himself to examine a Dino she was considering buying.

Daisy could hardly wait to break the good news to Chance and Sean, but she contained herself while another guest, a newcomer, purchased the dinosaur with the argyle socks.

"I didn't know anybody made stuff like this," he said. "Until I saw the photo in the paper, I thought modern art was just paintings, like Picasso."

"I hope you'll come to all our openings," Daisy said. "There's a lot going on in the art scene in Arizona."

By the time the last guest departed around five o'clock, three of the sculptures had sold. Visitors had expressed interest in two other works and promised to come examine them again.

Elroy was so excited his friend had to steer him out the door. Daisy pressed leftover cheese and crackers on them as they departed. "See? Free dinner, too," she joked.

While Sean and Chance helped her clean up, she told them about the gallery tour. "I can't believe they voted me in unanimously!"

"You deserve it." Sean carried the coffeemaker to the storage area for cleaning.

"I liked those pots from the start," Chance reminded her.

Daisy touched his wrist. "You're a good sport."

"What makes you say that?"

"You gave up a lot for me," she said. "You don't even seem to mind."

"Why would I mind?" He drew her close.

"Some men might," Daisy said. "After all, you could have been the one reaping the glory."

"You know what? I'm perfectly happy with my work the way it is," Chance said. "When I think about Washington, I feel as if I had a narrow escape."

Daisy relaxed against him, deliciously aware of the hardness of his body through her silky caftan. Then, abruptly, she got a jolt in the ribs.

"Hey!" Chance said. "You don't have to poke me."

"I didn't!"

"Well, somebody did."

"That wasn't a poke, it was a kick." She smoothed a hand along her abdomen. "Tom or Kitty is getting a little exercise."

"Really?" His face brightened. "That was the baby moving?"

"Giving you the stamp of approval," she said.

He caressed her bulge. The response was a gently rolling motion.

"He responds to my touch." Wonder filled Chance's voice. "He—or she—can hear me, too, isn't that what the doctor said?"

She nodded, filled with joy.

"I'm glad I didn't risk missing one single moment with the two of you," he said fiercely. "I want a whole lifetime full of moments like this."

"So do I," she whispered.

"How often do two people's dreams come true at the same time?" he asked.

Inside Daisy the baby snuggled down between its mommy and daddy. "Make that three people's dreams," she said.

Epilogue

Phoebe drifted through the water above the pool's intense blue tile. "Remember when we were trying to pick the colors for your wedding?"

Late-afternoon June sunshine dappled Elise's cheeks as she treaded water nearby. "How can I forget? You nearly drove me crazy."

Sitting on the steps in the shallow end with her daughter in her lap, Daisy said, "Thank goodness my colors were easy. Pink and blue!"

"They should have been red and green," Phoebe said. "It *was* Christmas Eve."

"Red and green for a wedding?" Elise shuddered. "I'm glad you didn't mention it at the time. I'd have beaten you to death with a sprig of holly."

Lucinda Foster, better known as Lucky, splashed her feet in the water with the enthusiasm of a healthy five-month-old. With her strawberry curls and chubby cheeks, she gave an angelic impression not entirely justified by her loud crying while teething the previous night.

Daisy hugged her daughter. She was more than happy to trade a little sleep for the adventure of motherhood.

The wedding had been everything she'd dreamed of. Her mother had designed a stunning ivory dress, and amid the pink and blue theme, Daisy's pregnant state had looked perfectly appropriate.

Although her father had promised to attend, she'd expected him to disappear at the last minute. But, amazingly, he'd been there, his long musician's hair neatly trimmed and his scruffy clothes exchanged for a suit. He'd said it was her mother's right to walk her down the aisle, but he'd stood in the receiving line greeting guests.

Mick couldn't make up for missing Daisy's childhood, but she didn't need him to. She had her own man now, one she could rely on without question.

Across the pool area, her gaze fell on Chance. He stood at the barbecue with James and Wyatt, looking relaxed. Since becoming a father, he'd been infinitely patient with Lucky and clearly happy in his life.

He'd taken delight last month in the fact that Daisy's one-woman show received rave reviews and drew record attendance to Native Art. The gallery tour in particular had been a triumph, with international interest focusing on her work.

"I hope we're going to eat soon," Phoebe said. "I'm starving."

"That's my line!" Daisy teased. Still breast-feeding Lucky, she wolfed down food as if a famine were due at any minute.

"The food must be nearly ready." Elise hoisted herself from the pool. "Then I've got a surprise for you all."

"Really?" Daisy said. "I've got a surprise, too."

"So do I!" Phoebe beamed at them. "No wonder we all couldn't wait to get together!"

"That's not the only reason," Elise said.

"Of course not," Phoebe agreed. "We miss each other, too, right?"

"Definitely," Daisy said.

Now that they lived apart, the three of them didn't see each other as much as in the old days. They phoned frequently and sometimes met for lunch at The Prickly Pear, though.

Both Elise and Daisy had moved into their husbands' homes. Phoebe and Wyatt had bought their adjoining second-floor condos and converted them into one giant unit. That way, they'd explained, they could spread out, yet still be near Wyatt's grandparents upstairs.

"Hamburgers are done," James announced. "Any takers?"

"Stand back!" roared Phoebe.

The three women snatched paper plates and buns from a side table. After collecting their burgers, they helped themselves to condiments, lettuce and tomatoes, three-bean salad and chips, then settled on chairs.

The men joined them, and for a while the conversation lagged while everyone ate. Elise broke the lull to say, "I'll bet I know Phoebe's secret."

"Phoebe has a secret?" asked James.

"Each of us has a secret," said his wife. "Now, look at the evidence. Unusually large appetite…taking next year off work to finish her degree…"

"What's your conclusion?" Phoebe challenged.

"You're pregnant."

"Are you?" Daisy asked, thrilled at the prospect.

Phoebe nodded. Shouts of joy went up from her friends, while the men offered congratulations. Wyatt sat beaming at his wife.

"We're over the moon about it, too." That comment

came from Helen Madison. Daisy hadn't seen Helen and Rolland approach on their evening stroll until they appeared, grinning ear-to-car over the prospect of becoming great-grandparents.

"I haven't forgotten how to change a diaper," added her husband. "We plan to do lots of baby-sitting."

"Oh, look how big Lucky is getting!" Helen said. The baby, who'd been squirming while Daisy tried to eat, responded to her name with a squeal. "Would you like us to take her for a walk?"

"I'd be grateful," Daisy said.

After the baby was tucked into her stroller and wheeled merrily away, the conversation resumed. "When are you due, Phoebe?" Elise asked.

"Early December. In time for Christmas."

"Your child will be less than a year younger than Lucky," Daisy said. "That's close enough to be playmates."

"If it's a boy, maybe we can make a match," Elise said. "That's one way of finding Mr. Right that Jane Jasmine didn't write about."

"Oh, please," Phoebe said. "I can't think that far ahead. I can't even think past childbirth classes."

"Get plenty of rest," Chance advised. "You'll need it." To Wyatt he added, "And be prepared to wait on your loved one. Like this." Without being asked, he fetched Daisy a glass of lemonade.

"Is motherhood really as hard as people say?" Phoebe asked Daisy.

She considered carefully before she answered. "It can be exhausting, but it's so exhilarating, you forget the hard times."

Also, in her case, the pregnancy had worked wonders for her endometriosis, so her health had improved.

She didn't want to mention that in mixed company, though.

"I hear Frannie and Bill are going to be parents, too," Elise said.

Everyone's attention riveted on her. "At their age?" James asked in astonishment.

"They're adopting a pregnant stray cat," Elise said. "She's due anyday now."

Rueful chuckles greeted this statement. "I should have known!" said her husband.

"All right, you've heard my surprise," Phoebe said. "Daisy, what's yours?"

Chance stretched his legs along a lounge chair. "Honey, don't keep them in suspense."

"I won't!" Daisy had been bursting to tell her friends the good news. "As a result of the gallery tour, I've been invited to be guest artist at a German symposium in October."

"Wow!" Elise said. "You're an international hit."

"That's quite an honor," noted Phoebe. "I'm proud of you."

"I get to go, too," Chance added. "Just think, Oktoberfest in Germany. We plan to do some touring after the symposium to enjoy the festivals."

"Think your clients can live without you?" asked Phoebe.

"I'll have another lawyer cover for me," he said. "I never knew life could be this pleasant. It beats the heck out of busting my brains in Washington, let me tell you."

His eyes met Daisy's. In them she read the things he wasn't saying in front of their friends.

How easily they talked about things now, and how

well they understood each other. How the more they shared their lives, the stronger their feelings grew.

"Who's going to watch Lucky while you're traveling?" Phoebe asked.

Chance cleared his throat. "The grandmothers are having a friendly battle for the honor. We'll let you know who wins."

"Okay, Elise," Daisy said. "Phoebe and I have come out with it. What's your secret?"

"I'm surprised I haven't heard about it, whatever it is," Chance added. "The family grapevine usually works fast."

"I haven't told anyone," Elise said. "I just found out yesterday."

"Found out what?" Phoebe asked.

Their friend gave a little bounce of excitement. "I sold my book!"

"What book?" said Daisy.

"It's a novel set in eighteenth-century France," Elise said. "The heroine is a noblewoman who's writing a book about 1800 ways to find true love. To do her research she embarks on a series of romantic adventures. Or misadventures."

"What fun!" Daisy cried. "You didn't even tell us you were writing one!"

"I didn't think it would sell," admitted their friend. "I hope Jane Jasmine doesn't mind serving as my inspiration."

"I think she'd be flattered," said Wyatt.

"We sure got a lot of mileage out of *her* book," said Phoebe. "Look, we all found husbands."

"Whether we were looking for them or not," said Elise.

"Whether we were ready to believe in love or not," added Daisy.

"Well, I think it's time she wrote a sequel," Chance said.

"About what?" Wyatt asked.

"How about, *2001 Ways to Raise a Happy Child*?" he suggested.

Heads nodded. "I'll buy a copy," Daisy said.

"Me, too," said Phoebe. "One of these days someone else whose name I won't mention might need it. Don't you think?"

Elise gave them a mysterious smile. "I'm willing to consider it."

"Really?" said James.

"Really."

He grinned.

A sense of deep satisfaction swept over Daisy as she listened to her friends share their hopes for the future.

The old days when she and Phoebe and Elise were practically inseparable had gone forever. But with the three wonderful men they'd found, they were moving into a future filled with challenge, excitement and joy.

For all the years to come.

*   *   *   *   *

Look for heartwarming author
Jacqueline Diamond's next emotional
love story, available September 2001, only
from Harlequin American Romance.

USA Today bestselling author

STELLA CAMERON

and popular American Romance author

MURIEL JENSEN

come together in a special
Harlequin 2-in-1 collection.

Look for

Shadows and *Daddy in Demand*

On sale June 2001

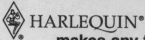

*Harlequin American Romance invites you to walk
down the aisle with three marriage-of-convenience
romances. These stories end with wedding bells and
begin with the most unexpected surprises!*

The highest bidder wins...a husband in
BACHELOR-AUCTION BRIDEGROOM
by Mollie Molay
June 2001

A town's matchmaking plans lead to startling results in
THE BEST BLIND DATE IN TEXAS
by Victoria Chancellor
July 2001

Enemies are forced to become Mr. and Mrs. in
COURT-APPOINTED MARRIAGE
by Diane Castell
August 2001

Available at your favorite retail outlet.